A Word from Stephanie
Younger, Older, or Just Right!

Why is life so complicated? Up until now, I had nothing but problems with boys. First, I liked Brandon, but he didn't like me. Brandon was two years older than me. When he paid me no attention, everybody said, "What do you expect from an older boy?" Then I liked Kyle. Kyle is one year older, but for a while, Kyle *did* like me. Then I found out that he's not so easy to get along with. In fact, dating Kyle was a major pain!

But then I met Dixon. Dixon is just right. He's cute and smart and *extremely* easy to be with. Going out with him is more fun than daydreaming about Brandon. And tons better than putting up with Kyle. So, what could go wrong? Everything! Because Dixon is two years *younger* than me. Major embarrassment. In fact, I can't let anyone find out. But keeping this kind of a secret is harder than I thought. How much harder? I'll tell you all about it. But not until I've told you about something that *isn't* hard right now. Being with my family. My very *big* family.

Right now there are nine people and a dog living in our house—and for all I know, someone new could move in at any time. There's me, my big sister, D.J., my little sister, Michelle, and my dad, Danny. But that's just the beginning.

When my mom died, Dad needed help. So he

asked his old college buddy, Joey Gladstone, and my uncle Jesse to come live with us, to help take care of me and my sisters.

Back then, Uncle Jesse didn't know much about taking care of three little girls. He was more into rock 'n' roll. Joey didn't know anything about kids, either—but it sure was funny watching him learn!

Having Uncle Jesse and Joey around was like having three dads instead of one! But then something even better happened—Uncle Jesse fell in love. He married Rebecca Donaldson, Dad's cohost on his TV show, *Wake Up, San Francisco*. Aunt Becky's so nice—she's more like a big sister than an aunt.

Next Uncle Jesse and Aunt Becky had twin baby boys. Their names are Nicky and Alex, and they are adorable!

I love being part of a big family. Still, things can get pretty crazy when you live in such a full house!

FULL HOUSE™: Stephanie novels

Phone Call from a Flamingo
The Boy-Oh-Boy Next Door
Twin Troubles
Hip Hop Till You Drop
Here Comes the Brand-New Me
The Secret's Out
Daddy's Not-So-Little Girl
P.S. Friends Forever
Getting Even with the Flamingoes
The Dude of My Dreams
Back-to-School Cool
Picture Me Famous
Two-for-One Christmas Fun
The Big Fix-up Mix-up
Ten Ways to Wreck a Date
Wish Upon a VCR
Doubles or Nothing
Sugar and Spice Advice
Never Trust a Flamingo
The Truth About Boys

Available from MINSTREL Books

Full House™
Stephanie

The Truth About Boys

Emily Costello

A Parachute Press Book

Published by POCKET BOOKS
New York   London   Toronto   Sydney   Tokyo   Singapore

This book is a work of fiction. Names, characters, places and incidents are products of the author's imagination or are used fictitiously. Any resemblance to actual events or locales or persons, living or dead, is entirely coincidental.

MINSTREL PAPERBACK *Original*

 A Minstrel Book published by
POCKET BOOKS, a division of Simon & Schuster Inc.
1230 Avenue of the Americas, New York, NY 10020

A PARACHUTE PRESS BOOK

READING Copyright © and ™ 1997 by Warner Bros.

FULL HOUSE, characters, names and all related indicia are trademarks of Warner Bros. © 1997.

ISBN: 0-671-00361-5

First Minstrel Books printing February 1997

10 9 8 7 6 5 4 3 2 1

A MINSTREL BOOK and colophon are registered trademarks of Simon & Schuster Inc.

Cover photo by Schultz Photography

Printed in the U.S.A.

The Truth About Boys

CHAPTER
1

◆ ◂ ✦ ◆

"How about this one, Darcy?" Stephanie Tanner held up an electric-blue dress covered with white ruffles.

Darcy Powell groaned. "I wouldn't wear that if you paid me a million dollars."

"They should pay us just for *looking* at it," Allie Taylor put in.

Stephanie giggled along with her two best friends. She was having a great afternoon. Shopping was always fun. But shopping for a fancy dress-up dance made it even better. There was only one thing keeping Stephanie from total bliss—the fact that she didn't yet have a date for the dance. She was getting a little worried about that. But the dance was still more than a week away. And the dance would be great, no matter who she went with. After all, Allie and Darcy would be there.

Stephanie and Allie had been friends for nine years. Their teacher sat them next to each other on their first day of kindergarten, and they were best friends ever since. Allie had gentle green eyes and wavy brown hair. She was a lot like Stephanie, but different too. For instance, they both loved music, reading, and funny movies. But Stephanie was also a great dancer, while Allie was pretty much a klutz.

"What do you think Justin will wear to the dance?" Allie asked Darcy.

Darcy had finally gotten up the nerve to ask Justin Foster to the dance. She still seemed surprised that he said yes.

Darcy got a dreamy look on her face. "Justin will wear something super sophisticated," she said. "And I have to find something super elegant, so we'll match."

Stephanie nodded. She hardly knew Justin, but she was sure he was as mature as Darcy said. He *was* in the ninth grade. And he managed and played drums in his very own garage band.

Allie was going to the dance with Zack Bach, a guy who sat next to her in history. Zack had curly brown hair and played left wing for the soccer team.

"What do you guys think of this?" Allie pulled a dress off the rack. It was white with black trim.

"Cute!" Stephanie said.

"You should try it on," Darcy agreed.

"Come back to the fitting room with me, so you can tell me what you think," Allie said.

The girls hurried to the back of the store. Darcy and Stephanie sat down on the floor outside the dressing room while Allie disappeared inside.

"Nine days until the dance," Darcy said. "I can't wait."

"Me neither," Stephanie said. "But I've still got to find a date."

"Don't get stressed out," Darcy said. "You can always go without a date. You might even meet someone cute at the dance."

"No way," Stephanie said. "You guys both have dates. I'd feel like a loser going without one."

"Then you'd better ask someone soon," Darcy told her.

"I can't ask anyone until I decide who to ask!" Stephanie argued. "This 'Girls Rule' dance is harder than I expected."

Stephanie liked the idea that girls asked boys to this dance. It was fun, being in charge that way.

Because waiting for a boy to ask you out was a drag. But it was an even *bigger* drag not knowing anyone she'd like to ask.

"Does Kyle Sullivan have a date yet?" Darcy asked.

"I don't think so," Stephanie said.

"You're *not* going to ask him, are you?" Allie called out from inside the dressing room. Her voice was muffled, as if she were pulling something over her head.

"No way," Stephanie said. "Besides, he's still mad about what happened on the ski trip."

Darcy nodded in understanding. During the trip, Stephanie had spilled an awful secret about Kyle: His middle name was Rufus. Stephanie didn't blame him for being angry.

"I can't believe Rene hasn't asked him yet," Darcy commented.

"Me neither," Stephanie said.

Rene Salter was Stephanie's archenemy. She was a pretty, popular, and *pushy* ninth-grader. Rene was also an important member of the Flamingoes— a group of the coolest, most popular girls at John Muir Middle School. The Flamingoes didn't really *do* anything but hang out together. And they always wore pink. Stephanie was invited to join their club back in sixth grade. But then she found out that the Flamingoes were pretty awful. They asked Stephanie to steal her father's phone card so one of them could make long distance phone calls to her boyfriend!

Stephanie could never do something so dishonest, so she quit. She and the Flamingoes weren't on very good terms anymore.

But Rene was also Stephanie's enemy because she and Stephanie both liked Kyle. Or used to. Stephanie considered Kyle just a friend now.

Allie emerged from the dressing room and twirled in a circle. The black and white dress was just above her knees. It was cut in at the top so that Allie's shoulders were bare. "What do you guys think?" Allie asked.

"It's perfect!" Stephanie told her.

Darcy frowned as she studied the dress. "I think it's too casual. This is a pretty fancy dance, remember?"

Allie admired herself in the floor-length mirror. "It's not so casual. It's elegant," she said. "I'm getting it!"

"Cool," Stephanie told her.

Darcy's eyes widened in horror. "Are you *sure?*" she asked Allie. "It's the first dress you tried on. What if you see something you like better later?"

Allie shrugged. "But I like this a lot."

"Well, if you're *sure*," Darcy said.

"I am." Allie disappeared back into the dressing room.

Darcy shrugged and turned back to Stephanie. "Why don't you ask Ethan Green to the dance?" she asked. "I think he likes you."

Stephanie made a face. "Nerd city."

"How about Kevin Thomas?" Allie suggested as she came out of the dressing room in her jeans and T-shirt.

"Kevin Thomas is way too popular," Stephanie said. "I heard three girls in the bathroom arguing over which one got to ask him first."

"Eddie Miller?" Darcy suggested as the girls walked to the register and took a place in line.

"Snooze-a-rama! No," Stephanie said.

"Well, you have to ask someone *soon*," Allie said.

"I know!" Stephanie replied. *Time for a subject change,* she told herself. "By the way, I talked to Uncle Jesse and Joey again last night. They can definitely deejay the dance."

Stephanie's uncle Jesse had lived with the Tanner family since Stephanie was five years old. He helped take care of Stephanie, her little sister, Michelle, and her older sister, D.J. Joey Gladstone was her father's best friend from college. Joey and Uncle Jesse were co-hosts of a radio show called *The Rush Hour Renegades*. Joey was always hilariously funny on the radio and Jesse knew more about music than anyone Stephanie knew. Allie, Darcy, and Stephanie were on the entertainment committee for the dance. Getting Jesse and Joey to deejay was their most important assignment.

"Celebrity deejays," Darcy said. "Very cool."

"They'll be great," Stephanie agreed. "The only problem is that having them at the dance will be almost like having Dad there." Jesse and Joey were like second fathers to her.

"I'm worried they'll do something to embarrass me," Stephanie added. "Actually, maybe it's best if I *don't* go to the dance."

"You have to go!" Allie wailed.

"C'mon, Steph—this dance is the biggest thing to happen at John Muir all year," Darcy said. "You *can't* stay home!"

"But what if I can't think of anyone special to ask?" Stephanie asked.

Allie accepted her shopping bag from the cashier. "I have an idea! You can ask my cousin Gus," she said.

"Gus?" Stephanie considered.

An image of Gus popped into Stephanie's

mind. Pleasant round face, straw-colored hair, brown eyes. His big passions in life were football and video games. Stephanie had known Gus practically as long as she had known Allie. He was nice and not bad-looking. But he was hardly special.

Allie saw the look on Stephanie's face. "Listen, why not consider Gus your backup date?"

"Good plan," Darcy agreed. "You can save Gus in case you get totally desperate."

"I guess it's not a bad idea," Stephanie admitted. But she didn't feel very enthusiastic about it. She wanted to be excited about her date to the dance. As excited as Allie and Darcy were. The idea of going with Gus made her want to yawn.

"Hey, let's look in here for you and Darcy," Allie suggested. She headed toward a store with some cute denim dresses in the window.

Darcy hung back. "That stuff is way too casual."

Allie gave Darcy an impatient look. "Where do *you* want to go?"

"Let's try Bettina's," Darcy suggested.

Stephanie raised her eyebrows in surprise. "Bettina's? I can't afford a pair of socks in there!"

"I know it's expensive," Darcy said. "But the stuff they have is very elegant."

"Whatever," Allie said with a sigh.

Stephanie felt a bit nervous as they headed into Bettina's. The place was just too quiet. No music. And no other teenagers either. The saleswoman shot Stephanie a disapproving glance over the top of her glasses. Stephanie stepped up to Darcy, who was carefully examining a rack of clothes.

"Let's hurry, okay?" she whispered.

Allie looked just as uncomfortable. "I feel like I'm in a museum," she whispered to Stephanie.

Stephanie giggled. The saleswoman immediately hurried over to them. "May I help you?" she asked with a forced smile on her face.

Darcy held up a straight skirt with a matching suit jacket. "Yes, uh—do you have this in a color besides *beige?*"

"Yes, that comes in a lovely sea-green tone," the saleswoman said. "Would you like to see it?"

"Uh—no, thanks . . ." Darcy's lips twitched. "Sea green makes me look—like a seasick mermaid!"

The saleswoman glared at them. Stephanie knew she was going to burst out laughing. She bolted for the door. Allie and Darcy were right behind her.

"Come on, you guys," Stephanie said. "I think she's about to call mall security. Run!"

Stephanie flew out the door—and slammed right into someone.

"Ouch! I didn't see ya' comin'," said a deep male voice with a slight southern accent.

"Sorry!" Stephanie said. She looked up—and felt her heart leap into her throat.

CHAPTER
2

♦ ◀ ▶ ♦

Stephanie was staring at a boy—a very cute boy. He had shaggy blond hair and green eyes with incredibly long lashes. And he was smiling at her.

"Are you—okay?" Stephanie stammered. She couldn't stop staring into his beautiful eyes.

"Sure," the boy said with a lopsided grin. "You were moving so fast, I couldn't stop in time. By the way, my name's Dixon."

Stephanie glanced at Allie and Darcy, who were standing a few steps away outside the door of Beats, the new record store. She felt funny talking to a stranger in the mall. But she didn't want to be rude, not after she'd practically flattened the guy.

"I'm Stephanie," she said.

This guy is too good-looking, Stephanie told herself. *He's even cuter than Kyle!*

Stephanie shifted her weight nervously. "Uh—are you from around here?" she asked, thinking of Dixon's accent.

"No," Dixon said. "I just moved here from Memphis."

"Weird!" Stephanie said.

Dixon gave her an insulted look. "Actually, it's a pretty *normal* town."

Stephanie smiled. "That's not what I meant. See, my dad works at a TV station, and his new camera operator just moved to San Francisco from Memphis."

"That *is* pretty weird!" Dixon exclaimed. "That's my mom!"

"Wow!" Stephanie said.

"Yeah," Dixon replied.

"So, uh—" Stephanie tried to think of something witty to say. "So—how come I haven't seen you at John Muir?"

"I'm going to Country Day," Dixon explained.

Country Day was a private school not far from John Muir. Stephanie had to fight back a smile when she imagined Dixon in a Country Day uniform. They wore white shirts, red ties, and navy blazers. Dixon was wearing a black T-shirt and baggy shorts. His look said "alternative rock" more than "prep school." He even had a hoop earring in one ear!

Darcy and Allie loudly cleared their throats.

"Well, uh, it was nice to meet you, Dixon," Stephanie said.

Dixon held Stephanie's gaze for a moment. *"Very* nice meeting you, Stephanie," he replied. Then he turned and started away down the mall.

"Wow," Darcy said, stepping up behind Stephanie.

Allie stared after Dixon as he walked away. "Too bad you can't ask *him* to the dance," she told Stephanie. "He's cute."

"You're right," Stephanie murmured. Dixon was adorable. And she was letting him walk right out of her life.

"I'm going after him!" Stephanie announced. Before her friends could react, she started running down the mall after him. "Hey, Dixon, wait up!"

Dixon turned around to see who was calling him. When he saw Stephanie, he stopped walking, a puzzled smile on his face.

Stephanie slowed down. Suddenly she wasn't so eager to catch up with Dixon. *What am I going to say?* she wondered as she closed the last few steps between them.

"Hi again," Dixon said. He looked friendly enough. At least he was smiling.

"Hi . . ." Stephanie swallowed. The blood was pounding so loudly in her ears that she could hardly hear her own voice.

"Why don't we get together sometime?" Stephanie blurted out. "I could show you around San Francisco." *Very smooth*, she thought in disgust.

"Oh," Dixon said. "Sure. Do you have a pen?"

"A pen?" Stephanie couldn't figure out what Dixon was talking about.

"So I can give you my phone number," Dixon explained.

"Oh—right!" Stephanie had come to the mall directly from school. She reached into her backpack and handed Dixon a pen and her math notebook.

Dixon wrote down his number. He hesitated before he handed the notebook back to Stephanie. "Do you think I could have your number too?" he asked.

"Oh! Sure," Stephanie said.

Stephanie concentrated on keeping her hand steady as she wrote her number, ripped it out of her notebook, and handed it to Dixon. He slipped it into the pocket of his shorts.

"If you don't call me, I'll call you," Dixon said. He hurried away.

Allie and Darcy rushed up to Stephanie.

"Awesome!" Darcy said.

"I am so impressed!" Allie added.

Stephanie stood up a little taller. "So am I! I can't believe I just did that!"

Darcy linked her arm through Stephanie's. "Now all you have to do is ask him to the 'Girls Rule' dance!"

"Hey, why not? You are talking to the bravest eighth-grader in all of San Francisco," Stephanie said. "Asking him to a dance will be absolutely no problem!"

Stephanie was still floating on air when she opened the front door to her house a half hour later. Even after she had walked her friends home, Stephanie couldn't stop thinking about Dixon. They had talked about him all afternoon.

She couldn't get over the way they had met. It was just so *romantic*. Like one of those movies where two people are destined to be together—somehow, they manage to cross the world and find each other.

"Hello, wonderful people!" Stephanie sang out as she entered the living room.

Jesse and Joey looked up from where they sat on the floor in front of the couch. They were surrounded by enormous stacks of albums and compact discs. Becky and the twins were settled into one of the oversized armchairs with a book. Michelle and Danny were putting together a jigsaw puzzle on the coffee table. Only D.J. was missing. Stephanie guessed that her big sister was holed up in her room. She had a big biology test coming up at school, and she'd been studying around the clock for days.

"Did you have a good time at the mall?" Danny asked her.

"The best!" Stephanie answered.

"Look, Steph," Michelle said. "I did the whole sky by myself." She pointed to a solid blue section of the puzzle.

Stephanie rumpled Michelle's hair affectionately. "That's great, Michelle. You are so clever!"

Michelle gave Stephanie a suspicious look. "Uh, thanks," she said.

"Hey, where did all of these old records come from?" Stephanie asked Joey and Jesse.

"The radio station let us borrow them," Jesse explained.

"We're planning what to play at your dance," Joey added. "We dug up some really great stuff."

"Yeah? Let me see." Stephanie sat on the floor next to Joey. Now that she had someone to ask to the dance, she was definitely more interested in helping to plan it.

"This is one of the great dance songs of all time," Joey said. He handed Stephanie an ancient-looking forty-five with a faded label.

" 'How Low Can You Go'?" Stephanie read off the label. "I've never even *heard* of this song."

"Well, it *was* recorded before you were born," Jesse told her. "But it's a terrific song. Trust us."

"Okay." Stephanie cast a doubtful glance at the rest of the records in the stack. She read off another record label. " 'Itsy Bitsy Teenie Weenie Yellow Polkadot Bikini'?"

"That's one of my favorites," Becky said, glancing up from her book.

"Really?" Stephanie asked. The song sounded silly to her. But Becky usually had pretty cool taste.

"Funny song!" four-year-old Nicky said with a broad grin.

"Funny," Alex, Nicky's twin brother, added.

Stephanie loved the twins. But she didn't think her junior high friends would like the same music as the preschool set.

"Don't you have any music that's a bit more— er, contemporary?" she asked her uncle Jesse.

Jesse was paying more attention to the records

than to Stephanie. "Look!" he said, pulling a musty album out of the stack. " 'Introducing the Beatles'!"

"Let me see that," Danny said. "Wow—I got this album for my twelfth birthday. It's one of the all-time greats!"

Okay, calm down, Stephanie told herself. She took a deep breath. "Uh, wouldn't it be fun to play some music that was recorded in this century?" she asked.

Joey gave Stephanie a wink. "Don't worry," he said.

"Right," Jesse agreed. "We've got everything under control."

"Well, but . . ." Stephanie started to protest. But then she remembered Dixon. She sighed happily.

"Sure," she told Jesse and Joey. "Whatever you guys decide is fine with me. I have complete confidence in you, and—"

She turned and noticed that her family was staring at her. "What?" she asked.

"You have a silly grin on your face," Michelle told her.

"What exactly happened at the mall today?" Becky asked.

"Nothing important," Stephanie said, trying to act casual. "I met someone, that's all."

"A boy someone, or a girl someone?" Becky asked with a knowing smile.

"A boy. The cutest boy ever!" Stephanie couldn't stop herself from going on. "He is cute and sweet and funny. And you'll never believe this—I ran into him!" she finished.

"Ran into—as in crash, boom, bang?" Danny asked.

Stephanie nodded. "Isn't it romantic?"

"Yeah," Joey commented. "Just like football—a really romantic sport. All those guys crashing into each other all the time. Who needs roses when we have the Super Bowl?"

Stephanie rolled her eyes. "I'm serious! I think destiny brought me and Dixon together."

"More like klutziness," Michelle said.

Stephanie frowned at Michelle. "I am not a klutz. And neither is Dixon. It was fate. We were meant to go to the 'Girls Rule' dance together," she added.

"Oh, I don't think that's a good idea," Danny said. "Even if Dixon *is* your destiny, he's also a stranger."

Stephanie gave her father a reassuring smile. "No, he's not," she told him. "He's the son of your new camera operator."

"Jennifer's son?" Danny asked. "But she just moved here from Memphis."

"So did Dixon," Stephanie replied.

"Oh! Well, if he's Jennifer's son, I guess there's no reason for me to object," Danny said.

"Thanks, Dad!" Stephanie jumped up to give Danny a kiss. The phone rang and Stephanie rushed into the living room to answer. "Hello?" she said into the receiver.

"Stephanie, hi! This is Dixon."

Stephanie's heart began to thump. "Hey, Dixon," she said as calmly as she could.

"Listen, I was wondering," Dixon began. "See, uh, I was thinking of going to the baseball game tomorrow night. But I have no one to go with."

"Really?" Stephanie asked. *I'll go, I'll go!* she thought.

"Yeah. So, want to give it a try?" Dixon asked.

"You mean, me go with you?" Stephanie swallowed. "Sure! I mean, okay. That'd be fine."

"Great! Now all we need is a way to get there," Dixon said. "My mom has to work late tomorrow."

"Well, meet me here. I'll find us a ride. No problem." Stephanie told him her address.

"Great! So, see you tomorrow," Dixon said.

"See you!" Stephanie hung up. She could feel herself grinning from ear to ear. Tomorrow night

20

Dixon would be right there, in her house. She could hardly believe it!

Suddenly she remembered Dixon's long hair and his earring. Her dad would freak if he saw those!

I'll meet Dixon outside and we'll get away before Dad even notices, Stephanie told herself. *After all, what Dad doesn't know won't hurt him.*

CHAPTER
3

◆ ◂ ▸ ◆

"Did you call him?" Darcy called to Stephanie the next morning.

Stephanie had just gotten to school. She bounded down the hallway toward Allie's locker, where Darcy and Allie were waiting for her. Stephanie could tell by the curious looks on their faces that they couldn't wait to find out what was happening with Dixon.

"No. But *he* called *me!*" Stephanie announced.

"Really?" Allie's green eyes widened and she shook her head in amazement. "When? What did he say?"

"When I got home, and nothing much." Stephanie answered, trying to sound as cool as possible. "He just asked me on a date—for tonight!"

"No way!" Darcy squealed. She covered her heart with her hand and slumped against the nearby wall. "This is so *romantic.*"

"I know," Stephanie said. "I feel like I'm the heroine in some romance novel."

Allie giggled. "I know just what the title would be. *Stephanie and the Hunk from the Mall!*"

Stephanie laughed along with her friends. But, actually, she thought Allie's title was pretty good. Dixon *was* a hunk.

"Are you nervous about tonight?" Allie asked as the girls started down the crowded hall toward Stephanie's locker.

"I guess I am a little nervous," Stephanie admitted. "I mean, the last time I had a date was with Kyle. I was so excited, and then we had such a terrible night. Both times we went out! But I have a feeling Dixon will be different somehow."

They all giggled, remembering how Kyle wouldn't let Stephanie make a single decision about their dates.

"No one could be like Kyle," Allie agreed.

The girls stopped at Stephanie's locker, and she turned the combination on her lock.

"Where are you going?" Allie asked.

"To a baseball game," Stephanie said.

"Was that Dixon's idea?" Darcy asked.

Stephanie nodded. "Yeah, but I think it sounds like fun."

"Did you tell your dad?" Darcy asked.

Stephanie nodded. "He was cool about it."

Allie sighed. "I'm so jealous. It's Friday and you have a real date. *I'm* baby-sitting tonight."

"And I'm *not*, for once!" Stephanie laughed. "Having a date with a cute new guy *is* pretty cool," she agreed.

"So, when are you going to ask Dixon to the dance?" Darcy wanted to know.

"I don't know. I'll have to wait for the right moment," Stephanie said. "After all, I just met him yesterday!"

"Well, I'm glad you're going to be at the dance," Darcy told her. "Because I really want you to see me in my amazing dress."

Stephanie turned away from her locker and gave Darcy a surprised smile. "You bought a dress?" she said. "But that's impossible. When we left the mall last night, you hadn't seen anything you liked."

Darcy shook her head. "I didn't *buy* one. I'm going to *make* one."

Stephanie almost dropped her math book. "*Make* it?"

"Absolutely," Darcy said with a confident smile.

"I learned how to do it while I was watching the Amanda Wong show last night."

Stephanie caught Allie's eye, and they both burst out laughing. Amanda Wong was a super house-keeper who had a weekly television show. On some shows, she whipped up incredible four-course meals. On others, she made all of her own Christmas gifts by hand. Stephanie's dad, who was a total neat freak, had taped an Amanda Wong special featuring her top thirty cleaning tips. He watched it at least once a month.

"What were you doing watching the Amanda Wong show?" Allie asked Darcy.

"I—I like it," Darcy stammered, clearly embar-rassed. "And besides, it's a good thing I *was* watch-ing. Amanda made exactly the dress I was searching for!"

"But, Darce—" Stephanie took a deep breath and chose her words carefully. "You've never sewn anything before!"

"That's okay," Darcy argued. "Amanda said *anyone* could make this dress in just four easy steps. Which is amazing because the dress is super sophisticated-looking. Exactly what I wanted. Any-way, I'm sure I can do it."

The bell rang, and the girls separated. Darcy hurried down the hall while Stephanie and Allie headed toward their homeroom together.

"I hope Darcy knows what she's getting into," Stephanie said to Allie as they slipped into their seats.

"You look pretty, Stephanie," Michelle said that evening. She was sitting on her bed in the room the girls shared, watching Stephanie get ready for her date with Dixon.

"But I don't understand why you're so excited about going out with a *boy*," Michelle added. "Boys can be so yucky."

Stephanie shook her head. "That's what you think *now*, Michelle," she said. "But just wait a few years."

But Michelle was right about one thing, Stephanie thought. She *did* look pretty. She was wearing her latest favorite outfit: a denim miniskirt with a wildly patterned shirt she'd found on sale at the mall. The outfit usually made her feel super confident.

But right now her stomach was doing backward somersaults. She was so nervous about her date with Dixon. What if they couldn't think of anything to say? Or what if he wanted to talk only about baseball?

Stephanie was also a little worried about introducing Dixon to her dad. What if Danny flipped out when he saw Dixon's earring? Stephanie's plan was to get Dixon out of the house before Danny even saw him. She figured it was her only hope.

Stephanie glanced at her watch. Ten minutes till seven. Dixon could be there any second!

"See you later, Michelle," Stephanie said as she rushed out of the room. She hurried down the stairs and headed into the living room.

"Hey, Steph," D.J. said from her spot on the couch. "Pretty cool outfit."

"Thanks," Stephanie replied. She was relieved that D.J. was ready and waiting for her. D.J. had agreed to drive Dixon and Stephanie to the stadium to see the game.

Stephanie was also relieved that Danny wasn't hanging around the door, waiting to pounce on Dixon when he arrived. There was still a chance she and Dixon could leave before Danny got home from work. With any luck, she'd get Dixon out of the house without introducing him to her father.

"Where's Dad?" Stephanie asked.

"I think he had a meeting after the show this afternoon," D.J. told her.

That's good news, Stephanie told herself. She

flopped down on the couch and started to flip through *San Francisco Scene* magazine.

"Hey, girls!" Joey's voice rang out. "What do you think of our outfits for the dance?"

Stephanie dropped her magazine with a start. "Joey!" she scolded. "You scared . . ." Her voice trailed off when she caught sight of Joey and Jesse, who were standing halfway down the stairs.

Joey and Jesse were wearing matching Hawaiian getups: baggy khaki shorts and shirts splashed with loud flower prints. Stupid-looking straw hats sat on their heads.

They both had their arms spread wide, with big goofy smiles plastered across their faces. They looked as if they had just finished a big dance number in some sappy musical.

D.J. started to laugh. "Outrageous!" she said.

"Okay!" Joey said. "D.J. obviously likes it. What do you think, Stephanie?"

"I think that if you wear those outfits to the dance, I'm dropping out of school!" she cried.

Jesse's grin disappeared. "I told you we looked stupid in these things," he told Joey.

"But that's the idea!" Joey protested. "I thought we would make the kids laugh!"

"Right," Jesse said. "But they'd be laughing *at*

us. Come on, let's see what else we can find. Wait right there, Steph."

Stephanie checked her watch. "Actually, Uncle Jesse," she started to say, "D.J. and I are about to leave and—"

"Don't worry. We'll hurry," Joey told her, bounding back up the stairs.

"This is so embarrassing," Stephanie told D.J. as soon as Joey and Jesse were gone.

D.J. shrugged. "Why? It's not like Dixon is going to see *you* in those outfits," she said.

"Well, seeing Joey and Jesse would be bad enough," Stephanie said.

She jumped off the couch and went to peek out the window. No sign of Dixon. And her watch said it was five minutes after seven!

"Where is he?" Stephanie wondered. She started to pace in front of the couch. "I don't know how much more of this waiting I can take."

"Wait no more!" Joey called. He strutted down the stairs, still dressed in his Hawaiian outfit.

"Now, this is cool, don't you think?" Jesse demanded as he appeared behind Joey.

Jesse had put together a hip-hop outfit: red jeans so huge they were hanging from his hips, the enormous sweatshirt D.J. usually slept in, and a pair of wraparound sunglasses.

29

"No way!" Stephanie said. "You can't wear that to my school!"

"Hey, isn't that my sweatshirt?" D.J. demanded.

"Yeah," Jesse admitted. "But I'm just borrowing it to give you an idea of the look I'm going for. It's the only sweatshirt in the house I could find that was big enough."

"So, what do you guys think?" Joey asked.

"Well—" Stephanie hesitated. "It's—uh, not exactly you, Uncle Jesse." *Thank goodness*, she added under her breath.

Just then the doorbell rang.

"It's my date!" Stephanie exclaimed. "Uncle Jesse, you've got to go change!" She ran at her uncle and chased him up the stairs.

"Okay, okay, I get the hint," Jesse shouted. "I'll try my old Elvis look next."

"I'll help you!" Joey cried as he hurried after him.

Stephanie flew down to the front door and stood there with her hand on the knob until Jesse and Joey had safely disappeared. Then she threw open the door.

Dixon was waiting on the doorstep. When he saw Stephanie, he broke into a smile that showed off an adorable dimple.

Joey and Jesse should ask Dixon how to dress, Stephanie thought as she smiled back.

Dixon looked fantastic in a T-shirt with a cool-looking snowboarding logo. The shirt was untucked over a pair of jeans and high-top Converse sneakers.

Casual, yet stylish, Stephanie thought.

She could tell Dixon had dressed especially for their date because his hair was still damp and neatly combed back. The way it was combed, his hair covered the little silver hoop in his ear.

"Hi," Dixon said.

"Hi," Stephanie answered, glancing nervously toward the stairs. "This is my sister D.J. She's going to drive us. So—let's go!"

"All right," Dixon agreed.

Yes! Stephanie thought as she waited for D.J. to scoop up her keys. *I'm actually going to get out of here without introducing Dixon to Dad!*

They left the house and started down the front walk. Suddenly Stephanie's heart sank. Danny was coming up the walk—and his eyes were fastened on Dixon.

31

CHAPTER

4

◆ ◂ ◆ ◾ ◆

Stephanie was trapped.

"Dad, this is my friend, Dixon." Stephanie crossed her fingers behind her back for good luck. "Dixon, this is my dad."

Dixon held out a hand. "Nice to meet you, sir," he said.

D.J. raised her eyebrows. "He's so polite," she whispered to Stephanie.

"Yeah. And Dad is big on politeness," Stephanie whispered back. He *had* to like Dixon now.

Danny gave Dixon a long, searching look.

At least Dad can't see Dixon's earring, Stephanie thought.

She squeezed her eyes shut. There was no telling

what her father might say. She imagined him telling Dixon that he wasn't dressed well enough to take Stephanie to a ball game. Or that it was unhealthy for him to be outside with wet hair!

"Well—" Danny cleared his throat.

Here it comes! Stephanie told herself.

"Nice to meet you, Dixon," Danny finally said.

Stephanie's eyes flew open.

Danny turned to her. "Have a good time, sweetie," he said.

"Uh—thanks," Stephanie stuttered. "Bye, Dad!"

"Bye!" Danny waited on the steps of the house and waved as D.J. pulled away from the curb.

"It's weird," D.J. said. "But I think he liked you, Dixon."

"Why wouldn't he like me?" Dixon asked.

Stephanie rolled her eyes. "My dad can be really overprotective," she explained.

Dixon shrugged. "Well, he seemed okay to me."

D.J. smiled at Dixon in the rearview mirror. "So how do you like Country Day?" she asked him.

Stephanie tried not to groan out loud. Why was D.J. giving Dixon the third degree?

Dixon didn't seem to mind. "Well, the uniforms are really awful. But they—I mean *we*—have a great baseball coach. So, that's cool."

"Are you already on the team?" Stephanie asked.

"Yeah." Dixon nodded. "You should come by and watch us practice sometime."

"Sure—that would be great," Stephanie said with a smile. Dixon had practically asked her on another date!

"Thanks for the ride," Dixon told D.J. as he climbed out of the car in front of the baseball stadium.

"You're welcome," D.J. said. "Call when you want me to pick you up after the game."

Stephanie slid toward the door. "Thanks, Deej," she said.

"He's sweet," D.J. whispered. "Have fun."

Stephanie nodded. She climbed out of the car and joined Dixon on the crowded sidewalk. There was a huge bunch of people waiting to file into Candlestick Park. The park was right on the water, and a strong breeze was blowing. Stephanie reached up to smooth her hair. Suddenly she felt really shy. What if Dixon guessed that she hadn't been on many dates before? What if Dixon went on dates all the time?

"The ticket line is right over there," Dixon said, pointing.

"Okay," Stephanie said.

"Let's get cheap seats," Dixon suggested as they stood in line. "That way, I'll have enough money for snacks too."

"Oh, I brought money for my own ticket," Stephanie told him.

"Really?" Dixon sounded delighted. "Great! Then we can get hot dogs *and* Cracker Jacks. I love Cracker Jacks. Especially the hidden surprise."

Stephanie smiled at Dixon. He was so easy to talk to! He really knew how to make his date feel at ease.

"I love Cracker Jack surprises too," she admitted. "The fake tattoos are my favorite."

Dixon broke into a grin. "Mine too!"

Stephanie and Dixon bought their tickets and climbed up to their seats just under the roof of the stadium.

"My granddaddy calls the cheap seats the peanut galley," Dixon told Stephanie. "He says that in the old days you could get seats up there for peanuts."

"Have you been to a lot of games?" Stephanie asked.

Dixon nodded. "Memphis doesn't have a pro team. But my granddaddy lives in Cincinnati. He takes us to see the Reds whenever we visit him.

But now the Giants are my home team! Only I don't know many of the players yet."

"Well, there's—uh . . ." Stephanie could feel her face turning red. "Actually, I don't think I know *any* of the players' names."

Dixon nodded. "You don't really like baseball, do you?" he asked.

"Well, it's not my *favorite* thing," Stephanie admitted.

"Then, thanks for coming with me," Dixon said. "Next time you should pick what we do."

Next time? Dixon wanted to go out again!

"Okay, I'll pick next time," Stephanie happily agreed. "The Star-Spangled Banner" started blaring from the loudspeaker and she prepared herself to endure a long, boring game. But to her surprise, the next few hours flew by. Stephanie and Dixon pigged out on junk food, did the wave, and even sang "Take Me Out to the Ball Game."

"Did you have fun?" Dixon asked. Stephanie had just called D.J. Now she and Dixon joined the crowd of people waiting to get out of the stadium.

"It was perfect," Stephanie replied.

"Well, except for the fact that the Giants lost thirteen to two," Dixon said.

"Right," Stephanie agreed with a laugh.

She was glad that Dixon was so into the game—even the silly parts. He looked totally cool, but he still knew how to have fun. Stephanie felt almost as relaxed with him as she did with Allie and Darcy. *And I can't wait to tell them about my perfect night*, Stephanie thought.

They followed the crowd down the spiral walkways that led to the sidewalk.

"Are you disappointed that we didn't get any fake tattoos?" Dixon teased.

All she and Dixon had found in their Cracker Jack boxes was a plastic car and a plastic ring. Stephanie was taking them home for the twins.

"Actually, I was super depressed," Stephanie joked.

"Maybe we'll have better luck next time," Dixon said.

Stephanie took a deep breath to keep her voice steady. Her heart was beating about a million beats a minute. "They have Cracker Jacks at the movies in the mall," she told Dixon. "Why don't we go tomorrow night?"

"Sure," Dixon said. "Thanks for asking."

Stephanie let out her breath in a rush. Things with Dixon were so easy. He was so nice. And so *cute*.

"There's your sister," Dixon said, pointing out the car. He grabbed Stephanie's hand and they ran toward the car together. They climbed into the car and Dixon started to tell D.J. about the game. Stephanie's hand tingled where Dixon had grasped it. She leaned against the backseat and sighed. No doubt about it—she was in love.

"Oatmeal or scrambled eggs?" Danny asked as Stephanie hurried into the kitchen for breakfast.

It was Saturday, and she had slept longer than she intended.

She stopped to think about breakfast. People in love were supposed to lose their appetite, but she was starving. "Can I have both?" she asked.

"Sure thing," Danny agreed. "Is Michelle coming down?"

"She was right behind me," Stephanie said with a nod.

Weekend breakfasts with her family were one of Stephanie's favorite things. This morning the kitchen was full of activity.

Joey was setting the table. Becky was getting Nicky settled into his booster seat. D.J. was helping Alex wash his hands. Jesse was handling the toast, and Danny was in charge of the cooking.

"Steph, could you help scramble the eggs?" Danny asked. He handed Stephanie a bowl.

"Okay," Stephanie agreed. "How many?"

"Uh—twelve should do it," Danny told her.

Stephanie went to the refrigerator and pulled out two dozen eggs. As she cracked the eggs into the bowl, she thought about Dixon and their date last night. She let out a dreamy sigh.

I wonder if Dixon will hold my hand at the movies tonight, she wondered. A shiver ran up her back.

Danny turned away from the stove. "Are those eggs ready?"

"Not yet," Stephanie said.

"Stephanie!" Danny exclaimed. "You really must be hungry! How many eggs did you make?"

Stephanie looked at the cartons that were sitting in front of her. They had both been full when she pulled them out of the refrigerator. Now they were both empty.

"Twenty-four, I guess," she said in a confused tone. "Why? How many was I supposed to make?"

Danny shook his head. "About half that! You must not be awake yet."

"I'm wide awake!" Stephanie exclaimed. "Well—maybe not," she added. She didn't want anyone asking her why she was acting like a flake.

"Scrambled eggs!" Michelle exclaimed as she rushed into the kitchen and took her seat. "Yummy. That's one of my favorites."

"Well, don't worry, Michelle," Joey said. "Thanks to Stephanie, we're going to have plenty this morning."

Danny planted a kiss on the top of Michelle's head. "Good morning, sweetie," he said. "Sit down. Everything is almost ready."

Michelle studied Stephanie as she climbed into her chair. "Did you have fun last night?" she asked.

Stephanie felt her cheeks flush as her face heated up. "Uh-hmmm," she mumbled, taking her seat.

"Did Dixon kiss you?" Michelle asked.

"Michelle!" Stephanie exclaimed. "It was our first date. And Dixon is a gentleman. And besides, it's none of your business."

"Did you want him to kiss you?" Michelle asked.

"That's enough, Michelle," Danny said. He dished out the eggs and then joined the others at the table.

"I almost didn't let you go, you know," Danny told Stephanie.

"Why not?" she asked as she poured milk on her oatmeal. She had almost forgotten how worried

40

she was, wondering what Danny would think of Dixon. That all seemed so long ago—like in another lifetime.

"Well, I did think that Dixon looked a little wild," Danny said. "His hair is awfully long," Danny explained. "And he has an earring!"

Stephanie glanced up from her food. "I didn't think you noticed that!" she said.

"I notice everything," Danny told her.

"Well, what's wrong with long hair?" Jesse asked. "I have long hair."

"Are you wild, Daddy?" Nicky asked.

"Like a wild animal?" Alex added.

Jesse caught Becky's eye and they both laughed. "Not quite," Becky told the twins.

"Oh, yes," Danny said. "When Jesse was a kid, he *was* pretty wild," Danny said. "That's why I wasn't going to let Stephanie date Dixon at first."

"What changed your mind?" Stephanie asked. "I mean, if you thought Dixon looked so wild, why did you let me go out with him?"

Danny shrugged. "I figured he was too young to get into too much trouble," he explained.

"Too young? I'm in eighth grade, and you're always worried that I might get into trouble," Stephanie said.

"True. But Dixon isn't in the eighth grade," Danny answered.

"He isn't?" Stephanie said in surprise. "He didn't tell me he was in ninth grade. Cool! So is Darcy's date for the big dance."

"Oh, Dixon isn't in *ninth* grade," Danny told her. "No, I thought Dixon was a safe date for you because he's younger than you. He's in the *sixth* grade," Danny said.

Stephanie almost choked on her oatmeal. "Sixth grade!" she sputtered. She started to laugh. "Cut it out, Dad. He is not!" she exclaimed.

Danny gave Stephanie a surprised look. "Well, that's what his mother told me," he said. "I don't think she was kidding."

Stephanie stared at her father. Then her eyes widened in horror. "You're still kidding, right?" she asked.

Danny shook his head. "I thought you knew," he said.

"Sixth grade!" Stephanie shrieked. "Oh, no! How *would* I know that?"

"Didn't you ask what grade he's in?" D.J. asked.

"No!" Stephanie wailed. "I just assumed . . . I mean, Dixon is so tall and cute—and way too cool to be in sixth grade!" She dropped her head into her hands and groaned.

Michelle sat up straighter in her chair. "What's the big deal?" she demanded. "You don't have to be *old* to be cool," she told Stephanie.

"It helps," D.J. muttered.

Stephanie glanced down at her plate and then pushed it away in disgust. There was no way she could eat now.

She was dating a younger boy! A *much* younger boy. What were her friends going to say?

CHAPTER
5

◆ ◀ ◗ ◆

"My turn to do dishes," Becky announced when the family finished breakfast.

"And I have to clear the table," D.J. said. "Who wants to help?" she joked.

"I'll help," Stephanie offered.

Becky and D.J. stared at Stephanie in surprise. "Great! I guess you should ask for help more often," Becky told D.J. "Thanks, Steph," she added.

"No problem," Stephanie said.

"Well, I'll help by getting the twins dressed," Jesse said as he picked up Alex.

"And I'll help you!" Joey told him. Joey scooped up Nicky, who squealed with delight as Joey trotted out of the kitchen. Danny and Michelle followed behind them.

"Wow. What got into this family today?" Becky asked.

"Actually, I wanted to talk to you guys alone," Stephanie told Becky and D.J. as soon as the others were gone. "I don't know *what* to do!" she exclaimed.

Becky turned away from the sink. "Do about what?" she asked.

"Dixon!" Stephanie exclaimed. "I can't date a sixth-grader. My friends will laugh at me!"

"Come on, Steph," D.J. said. "You're totally overreacting. A few years' difference isn't a big deal."

Becky came and put an arm around Stephanie. "D.J. is right," she said. "If you really like Dixon, you shouldn't let how old he is change how you feel."

"I *do* like Dixon. A lot," Stephanie said. "And I wanted to ask him to the dance. But—"

"But what?" D.J. prompted her.

"Well, last night Dixon was being really silly," Stephanie said. "He got all excited about eating Cracker Jacks and doing the wave."

"Sounds like fun," Becky said.

"It *was* fun," Stephanie agreed. "But now I'm

wondering—what if he acted that way because he's *immature?*"

"There's nothing immature about knowing how to have a good time," Becky said.

"Well, my friends won't want to hang out with a sixth-grader, fun or not," Stephanie declared. She slumped into a kitchen chair.

Becky pulled a chair up close to her. "Stephanie, you know that's not true. Allie and Darcy are better friends than that."

"Definitely," D.J. agreed.

"You just don't understand," Stephanie told them. "Maybe a few years doesn't make a difference when you're old, like you guys. But in middle school a year is a huge deal. And two is mega!"

"Well, try to be more open-minded," Becky suggested. "I bet that once your friends get to know Dixon, they'll like him too."

Stephanie sighed and stood up. "Sure. Right. Well, I have to go. I have a meeting at school." The dance committee was having a special Saturday meeting at John Muir that morning to make last-minute plans.

"Are you going to tell Allie and Darcy about Dixon?" Becky asked.

"I guess," Stephanie said.

"I know they'll say it's no big deal," D.J. predicted.

"Of course they will," Becky agreed.

"Over here, Stephanie!" Allie called. It was about an hour later. Stephanie had just walked into the cafeteria at John Muir.

Stephanie waved to Allie. She started to make her way across the crowded cafeteria toward her friends. Allie, Darcy, Stephanie, and their friend Hilary Dillon were all members of the entertainment committee.

"Hi, guys," Stephanie said as she joined the group.

"Hi!" Allie said. "So—why didn't you call us and tell us about your date?" she demanded.

"Uh, I was kind of tired," Stephanie said. "But it was—nice," she added.

"Nice?" Darcy repeated. "Come on—we want *details*."

Stephanie longed to tell her friends her awful news. But she couldn't exactly stand in the middle of the cafeteria and announce that she was dating a sixth-grader. She was relieved when she saw Kelly Myers storming across the room toward them.

"What's wrong, Kelly?" Stephanie asked.

"Rene!" Kelly exclaimed, shaking her head. "What else?"

Kelly was on the food committee with Rene Salter. Rene had been driving Kelly crazy for weeks. "Guess what Rene suggested we do now?" Kelly asked.

"What?" Stephanie said.

"She thought we should make forty dozen puff pastries—from scratch!" Kelly exclaimed. She shook her head in disbelief.

Hilary made a face. "Where did Rene get such a crazy idea?"

"From the Amanda Wong show!" Kelly exclaimed.

Allie, Darcy, and Stephanie looked at one another and started laughing.

"What's so funny?" Hilary demanded.

"I'm making an Amanda Wong dress for the dance!" Darcy said. She began describing it to Hilary as Christine Johnson, the committee president, called the meeting to order.

All the girls scrambled into their seats.

"So, Steph, was your date okay or not?" Allie whispered.

Darcy was sitting on Allie's other side. She leaned forward. "Yeah, what was going out with Dixon like?" she whispered.

"Well, something weird happened," Stephanie whispered back. "I'll tell you about it later. It's kind of personal."

For the next thirty minutes, Stephanie tried to forget about Dixon and concentrate on the meeting. But when everyone started arguing about what color balloons they should buy, her mind wandered. She couldn't wait for the meeting to be over. She needed to tell Darcy and Allie about her problem with Dixon. Waiting was driving her crazy.

"Okay, everyone, let's sum up," Christine finally said. "We decided on silver balloons, silver-and-white streamers, and ginger ale punch. Thanks for coming."

Hilary jumped to her feet. "See you guys later!" she said. "I promised my mom I'd be home half an hour ago."

"See you," Allie said. The others said good-bye too.

"Everyone on the food committee!" Rene shouted from the other end of the room. "Come over here for a second."

Kelly groaned. "I have a feeling this meeting is just *starting* for me."

"Don't let Rene boss you around," Stephanie told Kelly.

"She's not in charge," Darcy put in.

Kelly rolled her eyes. "*You* know that and *I* know that. But Rene just can't believe it. It doesn't help that our committee is full of Flamingoes."

"Move it, Kelly!" Rene shouted from across the room.

Stephanie gave Kelly a sympathetic smile as Kelly dragged herself across the room.

"So, talk! What happened last night?" Allie demanded as soon as Kelly was out of earshot.

Stephanie motioned for her friends to follow her into the bathroom. "Come in here—I'll tell you all about it."

When they got to the bathroom, Allie and Darcy pulled themselves up to sit on the sinks.

Stephanie was glad it was a Saturday. The room was deserted, and for once there wasn't anyone hanging around the mirrors.

"Did Dixon act like a creep or something?" Darcy asked.

"No, he wasn't a creep," Stephanie answered. She leaned against the wall facing her friends. "Actually, he was super nice."

"So what's wrong?" Darcy demanded.

Stephanie took a deep breath. "Well, I found out—and I really hope this isn't true, but I think it is because my dad told me—"

"Spit it out!" Allie said.

"Dixon's a little younger than me," Stephanie finally told her.

Darcy's eyes widened. "Really? He's only in the seventh grade?"

Stephanie stared down at her shoes. "Not exactly." She took a deep breath. "He's in sixth grade," she whispered.

Things got quiet. So quiet that Stephanie thought she heard a noise coming from one of the stalls. She shook her head. She was probably imagining it.

"I can't believe it," Allie finally said. "Dixon is so cool—and so cute."

"And tall," Darcy added.

"I know!" Stephanie exclaimed. "And he's mature too. Well, *pretty* mature. I was really happy about our date before I found out his age. And D.J. and Becky convinced me that a year or two difference in age isn't a big deal. But, well—what do you guys think?"

Allie chewed on her lip and thought about it for a second. "If you really like Dixon, I guess his age isn't important."

Stephanie smiled hopefully at Allie. "Then, you don't think it's a big deal?"

"Not if you really, really like him," Allie said.

"Great!" Stephanie breathed a sigh of relief.

"So, does that mean you're definitely going to ask him to the dance?" Darcy demanded.

"I guess so and . . ." Stephanie's voice trailed

off when she realized Darcy was looking at her as if she were crazy.

"Steph, you can't!" Darcy burst out. "Dixon is three whole years younger than Justin! Justin won't hang out with a baby like that. And then he won't want to hang out with me either!"

"That's crazy!" Stephanie said. "Why would he care who *I* go out with?"

"Because he *would*," Darcy insisted. "We'd all be at the dance together. Justin's in *ninth* grade. He can't hang out with some sixth-grader. You can't do this!"

"Well, what if Justin didn't know?" Stephanie asked.

Darcy looked at Stephanie in disbelief. "You mean you want us to keep Dixon's age a secret?" she asked.

"Well, I don't see why anyone else has to know I'm dating a sixth-grader!" Stephanie said. "Dixon goes to a different school."

"But what if someone asks?" Allie said.

"We won't answer. We'll change the subject," Stephanie told her.

"I don't like it," Darcy said. "It's too weird."

"Please, guys—won't you do this one little thing for me?" Stephanie pleaded.

"I don't mind, I guess," Allie said.

"Well—okay," Darcy said. "If you really want to ask Dixon to the dance, it's okay with me."

"Great. Then, Dixon's age can be our little secret," Stephanie said.

"No problem," Allie agreed.

"It better be a secret," Darcy said. "Because if this gets out, your reputation will be ruined, Steph. And since Allie and I are your best friends, people will think that *we're* complete dweebs too."

"Don't worry," Stephanie assured her. "That will never happen. I'll make sure of it."

"Oh, I think it's a little late for that," a voice rang out behind Stephanie.

Stephanie's heart almost stopped beating. She spun around. "Wha—" she started to say.

A girl with long black hair was standing outside the swinging door to one of the stalls.

"Wh—who are you?" Stephanie demanded. "How long have you been standing there?" Her voice came out in a squeak.

The girl stood there without saying a word. But two things about her told Stephanie everything she needed to know: Her bright pink T-shirt meant that she was a Flamingo. And her smirking smile meant that she heard everything Stephanie said about Dixon.

CHAPTER
6

◆ ◀ ▪ ◆

"You were eavesdropping on us!" Stephanie blurted out.

The girl shrugged. "You should make sure you're alone before you start telling deep, dark secrets." She laughed.

"Well, just don't tell anyone what you overheard," Stephanie told her.

The girl strutted over to the mirror and fluffed up her hair. "Sure. Maybe I'll tell just Rene," she replied.

Allie and Darcy shot Stephanie horrified looks.

"If Rene finds out about Dixon, she'll tell the entire school," Allie whispered to Stephanie.

"We'll be ruined," Darcy added.

Stephanie knew what the Flamingoes could do with a juicy piece of gossip. Last year they ruined the life of a quiet eighth-grader named Jasmine Andrews. The Flamingoes found out that Jasmine had repeated the fifth grade. Ancient history, right?

Not to the Flamingoes! They teased Jasmine about it in school, made up "funny" jokes about being left back, and even made phony phone calls to Jasmine's house about it. They made her life so miserable that she finally transferred to a different school just to get away from them.

I'd probably have to transfer to a school in Antarctica! Stephanie told herself.

She forced herself to look as calm as possible. "Go ahead and tell," she bluffed. "Rene won't care."

The Flamingo rolled her eyes. "Nice try. But all the Flamingoes know Rene can't stand you."

"Listen, er—" Stephanie began.

"Cynthia," the girl said. "Cynthia Hanson."

"Listen, Cynthia, I know all the Flamingoes, and I've never seen you hanging around with them anyway," Stephanie said.

"Well, I've been in the club only a week," Cynthia admitted.

"Wait a minute—aren't you in the seventh

grade?'' Darcy snorted with relief. ''You're not a very important Flamingo.''

An uncertain look passed over Cynthia's face. Then she frowned. ''I may only be in the seventh grade, and I may not be important *yet*,'' Cynthia admitted. ''But I think I just found a way to get Rene to notice me.'' She smirked at Stephanie. ''Even *I* wouldn't date a sixth-grader.'' She smirked again.

Stephanie felt her face heat up.

''You wouldn't dare tell Rene,'' Darcy blurted out.

''Why not?'' Cynthia asked. ''Why shouldn't I tell her right now?'' Cynthia turned toward the door as if she were going to run to Rene.

''Wait!'' Stephanie shouted. She exchanged a worried look with Darcy and Allie.

''You can't tell Rene,'' Stephanie said.

''Why not?'' Cynthia asked.

''Because, I—I'll make it worth your while,'' Stephanie told her.

Cynthia raised her eyebrows. ''Oh, yeah? How will you do that?''

''Well, I could do you a favor, or—'' Stephanie began.

''Will you give me that sweater?'' Cynthia asked,

pointing to the purple-and-white-striped sweater Stephanie wore tied around her waist.

Stephanie hesitated. "I just got this last week," she said. "I saved for months to buy it."

Cynthia shrugged. "Suit yourself," she said, starting to turn away. "I'm going to go see if Rene's still here."

Stephanie quickly untied the sweater. "Here," she said, holding it out to Cynthia. "Take it."

"Thanks!" Cynthia grabbed it enthusiastically.

Stephanie ached to rip the sweater from Cynthia's hands. But she didn't.

What's one piece of clothing compared to my life? she asked herself.

Darcy stepped up to Stephanie. "Steph, I think this is a big mistake," she whispered. "You just handed over your newest sweater!"

"What else could I do?" Stephanie whispered back.

Cynthia pulled the sweater on and admired herself in the mirror. "This looks great! Thanks," she told Stephanie.

The bathroom door swung open and Rene sauntered in. She stared from Cynthia to Stephanie and back again.

"Thanks for what?" Rene asked. "What's going on?"

"It's a bathroom," Stephanie told her. "What do you think is going on? Ballroom dancing? Bowling?"

Darcy and Allie snorted with laughter.

Rene ignored them and turned to Cynthia. "What about you, uh—"

"Cynthia," Cynthia said.

"Right, Cynthia." Rene repeated. "Flamingoes don't hang out with these losers, you know."

"Sorry, Rene," Cynthia said. "I just—"

Rene held up a hand to silence her. "That's a nice sweater. Where did you get it?" Rene pointed to Stephanie's sweater.

"I—I—I—" Cynthia stuttered. She looked to Stephanie for help.

"I lent it to her," Stephanie told Rene.

"Why?" Rene demanded.

"I don't have to tell you why I do anything," Stephanie put in. "I'm not a member of your little club, remember? But if you really want to know, it's because I accidentally spilled juice on Cynthia's T-shirt. She didn't want to be seen with a big stain on it."

Rene raised her eyebrows. "Really? Show me the spot," she ordered Cynthia.

"No!" Cynthia said. "I, uh—it's really ugly and I wouldn't want to gross you out. And besides, uh, I'm too shy."

Rene stared at Cynthia. "Fine, don't show me. But you're a terrible liar. I don't buy your story for a minute." She admired herself in the mirror for a moment and then turned to Cynthia. "Come on. I have a list of things for you to do for the food committee."

"But I'm not on the food committee," Cynthia protested. She followed Rene toward the door.

"You are now," Rene told her. The door swung shut behind them.

"Whew, that was close!" Darcy said.

"Too close," Stephanie agreed. She collapsed against the tile wall.

"Stephanie, you're crazy to let Cynthia blackmail you," Allie said.

"She's not blackmailing me," Stephanie protested.

"What do you call it, then?" Allie demanded.

"I did her a favor so that she'd do me a favor," Stephanie replied.

"Yeah, right," Allie said. "And I bet she thinks up a bunch more 'favors' for you to do by Monday."

"Don't worry," Stephanie told Allie. "I can handle Cynthia. After all, I handled Rene just fine. Compared to her, dealing with Cynthia will be a breeze!"

CHAPTER
7

◆ ◀ ◗ ◆

"Let's hit the fabric store," Darcy announced.

Stephanie swallowed a bite of her pizza and groaned. After the meeting, she, Darcy, and Allie had headed straight to the mall and the food court. "What's fun about a fabric store anyway?" Stephanie asked.

"Well, I might find the perfect material for my dress," Darcy said.

"And it has to be more fun than shopping in Bettina's," Allie added with a grin.

"You have a point," Stephanie agreed. She trashed the garbage from their lunch. "Let's go!"

Darcy led the way down to the first floor and out to the end of the long mall. Elinor's Fabric

Shoppe was sandwiched between an auto parts store and a tiny shop that sold hearing aids.

"I can't even remember the last time I was down here," Stephanie said.

"I don't think I've *ever* been in this part of the mall," Allie agreed.

"You guys make it sound as if there's something weird about buying fabric to make my own dress," Darcy complained.

"Not weird—just hard," Stephanie told her. "Are you sure you don't want to try on some more dresses?"

"Positive," Darcy said. She hurried into the store, and Stephanie and Allie followed her.

A woman with an elegant gray bun and glasses on a gold chain rushed forward, beaming at them. "Hello, girls," she said. "May I help you find anything special?"

"I need some fabric for a dress," Darcy said.

"Of course. We have some lovely dress fabric," the saleswoman said. She reached under a low table with both hands and pulled out several bolts of material.

Darcy glanced quickly at them. "Too pink, too patterned, too blah," she said, pointing to each bolt.

The saleswoman laughed. "I can see you have

something specific in mind. Why don't you look around by yourself. Let me know when you see something you like."

Stephanie gazed around the store. The walls were lined floor-to-ceiling with bolts of fabric.

"Uh, Darce—there are thousands of bolts of fabric," she exclaimed. "This will take forever!"

"We have time," Darcy said. "When do you need to be home to get ready for your date with Dixon?"

Stephanie ducked her head. "Shhh!" she warned Darcy. "Don't say that so loud."

Darcy and Allie both laughed. "There's no one around to hear us," Darcy pointed out.

Stephanie flushed. "I guess I'm a little spooked after what happened with Cynthia."

"I don't blame you," Allie said. "I think you should admit that Dixon is young and forget about Cynthia. Who cares what she thinks anyway?"

"That's crazy," Darcy told her. "Stephanie should just call Dixon and break their date."

"That's too mean," Allie cried. "Stephanie wouldn't do that to him, would you, Steph?" she added.

Stephanie frowned. "Well, no, I guess I don't want to be *mean*. But dating Dixon is turning out to be a lot of trouble."

"Well, it's worth it," Allie said. "Right, Steph?"

"I hope so," Stephanie answered.

Darcy turned and began to examine the bolts of fabric. She finally decided on a cobalt-blue cotton.

"How many yards do you need?" the saleswoman asked.

"I don't know," Darcy admitted.

"Why don't you let me see your pattern?" the saleswoman suggested.

"I don't have one," Darcy told her.

"Oh!" the saleswoman said. "Well, you'll need one. Why don't you look through these books and see what you can find?"

Darcy glanced at Allie and Stephanie. "Will you guys help me?" she asked.

"Sure," Stephanie said. She and Allie sat next to Darcy and started to flip through the pattern books. They were full of drawings or photographs of every type of dress.

"This is it!" Darcy announced about an hour later.

Allie and Stephanie leaned closer to examine the dress Darcy was pointing to. It had a full skirt that fell below the knees, tight long sleeves that came to a point over the hands, and a scalloped neckline.

"Pretty!" Allie said.

"Amanda Wong made *that* in four easy steps?" Stephanie asked.

Darcy nodded. "Sure. Well, at least something that looked a lot like this."

The saleswoman came over. She put on her glasses. "Pattern number four eight seven zero," she mumbled. She hurried off to search for the pattern.

"I'll make the dress this afternoon," Darcy announced. "Maybe you guys can come over tomorrow to see it."

The saleswoman came back shaking her head. "Sorry, girls, but we don't have that pattern in stock."

"Oh, no," Darcy groaned.

"Don't worry," the saleswoman told her. "I'll order it right now. It should get here in a few days. Give me a call on Monday, and I'll let you know if it's arrived. Will you take the fabric now?" she asked.

"Absolutely!" Darcy said.

The saleswoman cut the fabric and rang up the sale. Stephanie glanced at her watch. She was surprised to see how late it was. *Dixon's going to pick me up in only a few more hours,* Stephanie thought. Her stomach did a nervous flip-flop.

*   *   *

Dixon arrived at seven on the dot that evening. He was wearing jeans and a black ribbed T-shirt. He looked great as usual.

He really is tall for his age, Stephanie noted. *Probably the tallest boy in sixth grade. And no sign of baby fat.* She sighed. *He is young, but at least he doesn't look it,* she told herself.

"Mom's waiting for us in the car," Dixon said. "She'll drop us off downtown."

"Okay," Stephanie agreed. She followed Dixon down to the curb.

"Hi, Stephanie," Dixon's mom greeted her as she climbed into the car. She was a pretty woman with blond hair and green eyes like Dixon's. "It's nice to meet you," she said. "Your dad's told me so much about you."

"Nice to meet you too," Stephanie replied. She couldn't help wondering if everyone in her dad's office was laughing at her for dating a sixth-grader.

Dixon's mother drove them downtown. Stephanie had deliberately chosen a movie theater away from the mall. She figured there'd be less chance of meeting anyone she knew there. Dixon's mom promised to pick them up later, when Dixon called. She waved as she drove away.

"Your mom's really nice," Stephanie told Dixon politely.

"She's okay. So, what do you want to eat?" he asked. "Pizza, Chinese, or burgers?"

"Burgers," Stephanie said. "I know a great place nearby."

"Terrific," Dixon said as he followed Stephanie toward the restaurant. "I've been wanting to see *Freeway* for weeks," he added. "I'm glad you picked it."

"Me too," Stephanie said. Actually, she *had* been dying to see it. So that made the choice perfect— a movie she hadn't seen yet, playing at a theater far away from where most kids hung out.

Inside the restaurant, the hostess led them to a quiet booth near the back wall. Stephanie checked out all the booths—no one she knew. She breathed a sigh of relief and studied her menu.

"Brian Bayley is one of my favorite actors," Dixon told her. "Did you see him in *New Year's in New York?*"

"Yes!" Stephanie put down her menu. "My friend Allie and I saw that together. We usually like the same movies, but she thought it was really stupid."

"I thought it was great," Dixon said. "Especially the scene in the Statue of Liberty."

Stephanie started to giggle. "Or how about when he gets chased over the Brooklyn Bridge?"

"Classic!" Dixon said. "I read that there was a scene a lot like that one in *Freeway*. Only the new one is even more over the top."

"What do you mean?" Stephanie leaned forward and listened while Dixon told her everything he knew about the movie. The waitress came and took their orders. But Stephanie hardly noticed when her food came.

Dixon knew tons of cool stuff about actors and how movies were shot. They didn't stop talking the whole time they were eating. Before she knew it, the bill had come.

"Better hurry if we're going to make the movie on time," Dixon told her. He grabbed Stephanie's hand and pulled her out of the booth. He held on to it as they hurried down the street together.

Stephanie swallowed. It felt great, holding Dixon's hand and walking beside him. She had to practically run to keep up with his long stride. They made it to the theater and quickly bought tickets.

"Perfect timing!" Dixon said. He handed their tickets to the usher. "The movie is just about to start."

"Don't forget that we need to buy Cracker Jacks," Stephanie joked. She pointed to the snack line.

"I'd never forget that," Dixon told her. "I'm counting on tattoos this time. Hey—I think one of your friends is waving at us."

Allie and Darcy are here? Stephanie thought in confusion. She glanced up, and spotted Cynthia, waving across the lobby! She was standing with Rene and a flock of their Flamingo friends. And she was wearing Stephanie's sweater!

Uh-oh! Stephanie thought. *My secret is about to go public!*

"Come on," she cried, grabbing Dixon's arm. "Let's find seats—now!"

"Well, don't you want to say hi to your friend?" Dixon asked. "She's coming right over."

Cynthia rushed across the lobby toward them.

"Please let's sit down," Stephanie begged Dixon. "I, uh—er, my legs are really tired."

Dixon smiled at Stephanie. Obviously, he thought she was still joking. "I refuse to sit down without my Cracker Jacks," he joked back.

They had finally reached the front of the line. "Two boxes of Cracker Jacks, please," Dixon told the woman behind the counter.

"Hey, Stephanie," Cynthia exclaimed as she reached them. "What a coincidence! Rene and I were just talking about you."

Stephanie's eyes widened in horror. "You were? But, don't forget, you promised—"

"Rene was just saying that the entertainment at the dance had better be good," Cynthia said.

"Oh! Well, it will be," Stephanie answered. She forced a smile and took a deep, calming breath. *It's all right*, she told herself. *Cynthia didn't tell. Yet.*

"Well—see you later," Stephanie said. She gave Cynthia a get-lost look.

"Wait! Aren't you going to introduce me to your date?" Cynthia asked. She smiled.

Stephanie didn't say anything, but Dixon smiled back at Cynthia. "Hi, I'm Dixon," he said.

"Cynthia," she replied.

"So, are you here with your parents?" Cynthia asked.

Dixon gave her a puzzled look. "Why would I bring them on a date?"

"Oh, I don't know," Cynthia replied. "I thought maybe this movie was rated PG-13."

"I don't get it," Dixon said as he took back his change.

"It's an inside joke," Cynthia told him. She tried not to burst out laughing.

Stephanie glanced around. She almost choked when she saw Rene! She was walking right toward them.

"Well, let's go in," Stephanie said, pulling on Dixon's arm.

"Hey, Stephanie." Rene glanced at Cynthia. "What are you two talking about *this* time?"

"Stephanie told me that Dixon just moved here," Cynthia answered. "I wanted to welcome him to San Francisco."

Rene stared at Dixon. She blinked and her expression changed. She seemed friendly. *Very* friendly.

"Hi, Dixon! So, where are you going to school?" Rene gave him a bright smile.

"Country Day," Dixon told her.

Please don't let her ask him what grade he's in! Stephanie thought.

"Really? I have a friend who goes there," Rene said. "Do you know Michael Allen?"

"Uh—I don't think so," Dixon said.

That's probably because Michael Allen isn't in the sixth grade! Stephanie thought. "Well, see you guys at school," she said out loud. She tried to pull Dixon inside the movies. But he was too polite to walk away.

"So, Dixon, do you have lots of school dances at Country Day?" Rene asked.

"None so far," Dixon told her. "But I've been there only a week."

"Oh. Well, I just wondered if you were coming to the 'Girls Rule' dance at our school," Rene said.

Dixon shrugged. "Sounds like fun, but Stephanie hasn't asked me yet."

"Really?" Rene blinked as if she were surprised. She turned to Stephanie. "What are you waiting for?"

Stephanie didn't know what to do. If she didn't ask Dixon now, Rene would be awfully suspicious. And Allie would think she was super mean. Plus, it would really hurt Dixon's feelings.

But if she *did* ask him, Cynthia would be blackmailing her for the rest of her life! And Darcy might never forgive her!

Just be cool, Stephanie told herself.

She turned to Dixon with a big smile. "Want to go to the dance with me?" she asked. "It's next Saturday night."

Please, be busy on Saturday night, she thought.

"I'd love to," Dixon told her with an adorable grin.

"Maybe I'll see you there," Rene said. She flashed Dixon a big smile, then turned and hurried back to her friends. Cynthia ran after her.

"Your friends seem nice," Dixon said to Stephanie. "I'm glad Rene made you ask me to the dance."

"Yeah. Me too," Stephanie said. She wished she *were* glad. But she kept imagining herself at the dance, trying to keep Dixon's age a secret while Rene and the other Flamingoes asked him a million questions. Impossible! Dixon was too polite *not* to answer a question. If anyone asked what grade he was in, he would tell. And there was no way she could tell him *not* to tell.

I'm dead! she thought to herself.

CHAPTER
8

◆ ◢ ◆ ◢ ◆

"Yo, Stephanie! Wait up!"

Even before Stephanie turned around to see who was calling her, she knew that voice. Cynthia.

Stephanie turned away from her locker and met Cynthia's gaze. "What do you want?" she asked.

Cynthia gave Stephanie a brilliant smile. "Guess what? I was just talking to Mary Kelly," she said. Mary was a seventh-grade Flamingo. "She told me she was in your math class last year."

"So?" Stephanie asked, confused.

"So Mary says you got straight A's," Cynthia went on.

"And why was Mary so thrilled about that?" Stephanie asked.

"She couldn't care less," Cynthia admitted. "But I do. See, I'm flunking math."

"That's not my problem," Stephanie said.

"It is now," Cynthia said. "That is—unless you want everyone to know that you're going to the dance with a *sixth*-grader."

"But you promised not to tell," Stephanie reminded Cynthia.

"And *you* promised to do whatever I asked," Cynthia said. She held out her algebra book. "We have to do the problems at the end of Chapter Three for tomorrow. Bring them by my locker before school."

Stephanie shook her head. "I can't do your algebra problems. I haven't even thought about algebra since school let out last year. In case you've forgotten, I'm taking geometry now."

"Then I guess you'll have to review," Cynthia said. "And fast. Because I have algebra homework *every* night."

Stephanie hesitated.

"Sixth grade," Cynthia reminded her.

"Oh, all right!" Stephanie snatched the textbook out of Cynthia's hand.

"And while we're here . . ." Cynthia rooted around in her backpack. She pulled out her smelly, wadded-up gym clothes and tossed them to Steph-

74

anie. "Wash those before tomorrow," Cynthia ordered. "By hand. I don't want them to shrink in the washer-dryer. And don't forget to use fabric softener."

Stephanie's mouth dropped open. "Who do you think I am—your slave?" she demanded.

Cynthia smiled sweetly. "That's *exactly* who I think you are. I can't wait to dream up your *next* orders! Bye now!"

Stephanie stood staring as Cynthia disappeared around the corner. Then she collapsed against the locker with a groan.

This is unbelievable! she thought. *Cynthia is going to ruin my life!*

"Here's your math homework," Stephanie told Cynthia. It was the next morning and she had raced to catch up with Cynthia in front of Cynthia's locker.

Cynthia flipped through the homework. "Where's the second page?" she asked, scowling.

"On the back," Stephanie snapped. She'd spent an hour the night before reviewing Cynthia's textbook before she even began the problems. By the time she finished page one, she was steaming. You were supposed to write the answers on separate pages, but by then she wasn't about to use an extra piece of paper to make Cynthia's homework look good.

"These answers better be right," Cynthia warned her.

"Listen, I did my best," Stephanie said. Actually, she had purposely answered wrong on every other answer. "But I don't think you want to start getting perfect papers right away. Your teacher might think something strange was going on."

"Well, okay. But I want tonight's assignment to be perfect," Cynthia told her.

Stephanie frowned. "I hope you don't expect me to do your math homework for the rest of the year," she said.

"Why not?" Cynthia answered. "And just so you know, my English class is doing a big research paper next month." She smiled at Stephanie. "Now, where are my gym clothes?"

"Here," Stephanie said, pulling them out of her backpack.

"It's a good thing you didn't forget these," Cynthia said, grabbing her clothes out of Stephanie's hand.

"You're welcome," Stephanie told her sarcastically.

Cynthia ignored her. She examined her clothes carefully. "Hey—these are still damp!"

"Oh, did you want them dried?" Stephanie asked. "You didn't mention that. You just said to wash them."

Cynthia's eyes narrowed. "You did this on purpose!"

"Really? What are you going to do about it?" Stephanie asked with a shrug.

Cynthia thought for a moment. "I'm going to punish you," she declared. "I want you to apologize—by kissing my feet."

"Get real!" Stephanie exclaimed. She stared down at Cynthia's pink Converse sneakers. "I won't!"

"You will, or—" Cynthia began to say.

Just then the bell rang. The crowd in the hallway started to thin out as kids rushed to their homerooms.

"I've got to run," Stephanie told Cynthia, turning to go.

"Okay, have it your way," Cynthia said. Her eyes scanned the hallway—and landed on Darah Judson. Darah was a ninth-grade Flamingo. And one of Rene's best friends!

"Hey—Darah!" Cynthia called.

"Don't!" Stephanie gasped. Telling the secret to Darah was practically the same thing as telling Rene.

Cynthia smiled. "Then kiss my feet," she demanded.

Stephanie took a deep breath. Then she quickly bent her knees a bit and kind of blew a kiss at Cynthia's sneakers. When Stephanie stood up, Darah was standing right in front of her, looking puzzled.

"Stephanie?" Darah asked. "What were you just doing?"

"I—uh, I was looking for Cynthia's earring," Stephanie said. "Right, Cynthia?"

Cynthia opened her mouth, but then clamped her lips together as if she were trying to keep herself from bursting out laughing. She nodded at Darah.

Darah didn't look as if she believed Stephanie or Cynthia. "Yeah—right," Darah said. "Well, see you at the bake sale tomorrow, Cynthia," she added as she headed down the hall. "Don't forget the cookies."

As soon as Darah was gone, Cynthia burst out laughing. "That was great! Imagine. A few days ago I was a lowly seventh-grader. Now I can make an eighth-grader do whatever I want."

Stephanie rolled her eyes. "May I go now, your evil majesty?" she asked. "I won't have time to do your homework if I get detention for being late to class."

"Not yet," Cynthia said. "I have another assignment for you. You heard Darah—the Flamingos are having a bake sale tomorrow."

"So?" Stephanie asked.

"So Rene told me to make six dozen chocolate chip cookies," Cynthia said. "You can bring them by the front hall after school tomorrow. Oh, and make sure you make them from scratch. Rene doesn't like those kind that come in a roll."

Stephanie almost laughed out loud. For one thing, she never wanted to bake again. Not after her crazy attempt to start a catering business. But the idea of her raising money for the Flamingoes was totally ridiculous.

But what's more ridiculous is that I'm going to do it, Stephanie thought. She just had to get rid of Cynthia and her blackmail scheme!

And there was only one way to do that: Get rid of Dixon. And fast!

CHAPTER
9

◆ ◣ ◢ ◆

"So, will you guys help me?" Stephanie asked. Darcy and Allie climbed onto the bus after her.

They were on their way home after school.

"No way," Allie said as she took her seat.

Stephanie glanced at her in surprise.

"Sorry," Allie said. "But I still think it's really nasty of you to dump Dixon because of the Flamingoes. Besides, who else will you take to the dance?"

"Listen, I can't worry about the dance now," Stephanie said.

Stephanie waited until Darcy was settled in her seat before she continued.

"But I've got to find a way to get rid of Dixon," she added.

"I thought you had a great time with him the other night," Allie said.

Stephanie couldn't stop herself from smiling. "I did. And I don't want to hurt his feelings, but—"

"But you're tired of kissing Cynthia's shoes," Darcy supplied.

"Exactly!" Stephanie heaved an enormous sigh. "I really wish Dixon were older. But he's not. So I have to do this. If I don't, Cynthia will ruin my life."

"Well, I'll help you," Darcy offered.

"You will?" Stephanie said. "That's great! So what do you think I should do?"

"Easy. Use an excuse, like, you can't go to the dance at all, because, uh, your grandmother is visiting from Cleveland. No—from Russia," Darcy said. "That sounds more important."

Allie groaned. "Or how about an aunt from Albania," she added. "That is so lame!"

"Come on, you guys," Stephanie said. "This is serious. I can't use a dumb excuse!"

"Don't worry," Darcy said, patting Stephanie on the shoulder. "I'll think of something else later. I'm good at making up excuses under pressure."

"Well, it can't be too much later," Stephanie said. She sat back against her seat.

"Why? When are you planning to do this?" Allie asked.

"As soon as possible," Stephanie told her. She turned to Darcy. "Dixon has baseball practice this afternoon. We should go over to the field and talk to him today."

"Okay," Darcy said with a nod. "We might as well get it over with."

Stephanie glanced at her watch. "Country Day doesn't get out for another hour."

"That's perfect!" Darcy said. "Then both you guys can stop at my house first and see what I've done on my dress."

Allie looked puzzled. "I thought the woman at the fabric store said the pattern wasn't coming in until today."

"It's not," Darcy said. "Hey, come on, this is my stop!"

Darcy grabbed her books and jacket and raced off the bus. Stephanie and Allie jumped up to follow her.

"Hurry, you guys!" Darcy called.

Stephanie and Allie caught up to Darcy on the corner. "Wait, Darcy," Stephanie said. "I don't get it—what are we going to look at?"

"I cut out my dress!" Darcy said.

"Without the pattern?" Allie asked.

"Why not?" Darcy replied as they crossed the street and headed toward her house.

"Because the lady at the fabric shop said you needed a pattern," Allie reminded her.

Darcy shrugged as she unlocked the front door of her house. "Amanda Wong didn't use a pattern," she argued. "I think you need one only if you're not sure how you want the dress to look. And I know *exactly* how I want mine to look."

Stephanie and Allie followed Darcy upstairs to her room. A sewing machine was sitting on her desk. The bed was neatly made and Darcy had carefully laid pieces of material out on it. Stephanie thought the pieces looked a little strange, but she didn't tell Darcy that.

Allie carefully picked up a very long piece of material that ended in a point. "What's this?" she asked.

"That's a sleeve," Darcy said. "Remember? The dress has long sleeves that come to a point over my hands."

"My mother's wedding dress had sleeves like that," Allie said. "And she had a formal wedding."

"This dress *is* very formal," Darcy said. "I'm making it floor-length."

Stephanie and Allie looked at each other in surprise.

"Uh, Darce—" Stephanie said carefully. "Won't you be too dressed up for the gym?"

"No!" Darcy said with a stubborn shake of her head. "I want to look elegant and grown-up. After all, I am going with a *ninth*-grader."

"Speaking of our dates, we'd better go over to the baseball field," Stephanie said. "I really want to get this over with."

"Are you *sure* you want to dump Dixon?" Allie asked her.

Stephanie hesitated. "As sure as I'll ever be," she said.

Allie started to say something else, but Stephanie held up a hand.

"Don't try to talk me out of this," she told Allie. "I've made up my mind. Besides, there's no other way out."

"Ready?" Stephanie asked. She and Darcy waited outside the ball field at Country Day.

They could see about twenty boys spread out across the baseball diamond in front of them. Spotting Dixon was easy. He stood about a foot taller than his teammates. Next to him, they looked like *babies*.

"There's Dixon near third base," Stephanie said. "Throwing a ball to that short kid with freckles."

"They're all short, next to Dixon," Darcy murmured. She stared. "Wow. I guess Dixon is friends with these guys. Weird, isn't it?" she asked Stephanie.

"I'd rather not think about it," Stephanie replied.

"Good thing Dixon never suggested a double date with his sixth-grade pals," Darcy went on with a laugh. "That could have been really embarrassing."

Stephanie grabbed Darcy's arm. "Hey, you're here to *help* me, remember? Now, come on—let's do this and get out of here before anyone we know sees us."

"Good idea," Darcy agreed.

Stephanie and Darcy hurried across the field. Just then Dixon looked up and caught sight of them.

"Look—Dixon spotted us," Stephanie said. She watched as he tossed the ball to his partner and trotted their way.

"I'm so nervous!" Stephanie whispered to Darcy.

Darcy put an arm around Stephanie's shoulder. "Don't worry," she said. "I'll take care of everything!"

Stephanie nodded. She took a deep breath and let it out slowly. It didn't do much to calm her nerves.

"Hi, Steph!" Dixon's face lit up with a brilliant smile as he reached them. "What are you doing here?"

Stephanie met Dixon's green eyes. It was strange, but she couldn't help feeling pleased that Dixon was paying so much attention to her. Sixth-grader or not, he was awfully cute.

"Well, I, er—" Stephanie shot a quick look at Darcy. *Say something*, she pleaded silently. But Darcy was staring at Dixon with a stupid grin on her face.

Stephanie cleared her throat. "Dixon, this is my friend Darcy. She was at the mall that day, when we met."

"Oh, sure. Hi, Darcy!" Dixon said.

"Hi," Darcy echoed.

Stephanie waited for Darcy to add something. *Anything*. Even if it was something as dumb as the excuse about Stephanie's grandmother visiting from Russia. But Darcy said nothing. She just grinned up at Dixon.

"So, you didn't answer my question," Dixon reminded Stephanie. "Why are you here?"

"Uh, we were on our way home from school and, well, we thought we'd see how your practice was going," Stephanie finally said.

"It hasn't really started yet," Dixon told her.

"But I'm glad you came by." He glanced at Darcy and lowered his voice. "I was going to call you tonight and tell you how much fun I had on Saturday."

"Oh! That's nice," Stephanie said, feeling awkward.

"I also wanted to ask you what I should wear to the dance," Dixon added.

"Dance?" Stephanie repeated. She nudged Darcy in the ribs. If she was going to come up with some brilliant reason Stephanie couldn't go, now was the time.

Darcy didn't move. Stephanie stepped on her foot—hard.

"Ow!" Darcy yelped. "Oh, the dance—well, it's pretty formal. My date is wearing a jacket and a tie."

"No problem," Dixon said. "I wear a jacket and tie to school every day."

"Great," Darcy said. "You'll look nice."

Dixon smiled at Darcy, then turned to Stephanie again. "I better go warm up before Coach gets here. Give me a call soon, okay?"

"Uh, okay," Stephanie agreed.

Dixon headed back toward third base.

As soon as he was gone, Stephanie turned furiously to Darcy. "How could you *do* that?" she cried. She stomped off the field.

Darcy hurried after her. "Do what? Wait, Steph," she called.

Stephanie spun around to face her. "Do *what?*" she repeated. "Do *what?* Didn't you forget something? Like getting me out of this date?"

"Oh, well," Darcy began. "I wasn't sure you still wanted me to do it."

"But that's why we came down here, remember?" Stephanie asked.

"I know, I know," Darcy replied. "But once I saw you with Dixon, I wasn't sure you still wanted to go through with it."

"Why not?" Stephanie demanded.

"Because! You seemed so happy when he was talking to you," Darcy said. "I mean, your face turned bright red the minute he looked at you. And he looked really adorable in his baseball uniform."

"Yeah, he did look cute," Stephanie admitted. "But he's still in the sixth grade!"

"I know," Darcy agreed. "And those *other* sixth-graders are pathetic. But you guys seemed so perfect together. I don't know, maybe Allie is right. Maybe Dixon is a special case. Maybe you shouldn't let the Flamingoes ruin it for you."

"That's easy for you to say!" Stephanie exclaimed. "You don't have to do Cynthia's algebra homework when you get home. And you don't have to bake cookies for the Flamingoes' stupid bake sale either. No boy is worth all that!"

"I don't know what you should do," Darcy confessed. "What if I broke your date and then you changed your mind?"

"Well, what about Justin, your big date?" Stephanie asked back. "What about you saying that Justin wouldn't be caught dead with Dixon?"

Darcy shrugged. "Well, if Justin doesn't know, he won't care," she said. "Dixon doesn't *look* young."

"I can't believe this!" Stephanie stared at Darcy. "You were the one who told me to dump Dixon!"

"I'm sorry," Darcy said in a helpless tone of voice.

"Fine," Stephanie said. "I'll dump Dixon myself. He may be cute, but enough is enough. No way will I be Cynthia's slave for the rest of my life!"

CHAPTER
10

◆ ▼ ◆ ◆

"Mmm, chocolate chip—my favorite," Joey said. He picked up a spoon and dug a hunk of batter out of the bowl Stephanie was stirring.

Stephanie grabbed the bowl away. "Cut that out!" she told him. It was after dinner and she was almost done mixing batter for tomorrow's bake sale.

Jesse snuck up on Stephanie's other side and grabbed a spoonful of dough for himself.

"Two against one," Stephanie complained. "No fair."

"This is delicious," Jesse mumbled with his mouth full.

"Absolutely," Joey agreed.

Stephanie stuck her finger into the bowl and licked it. It *was* good. But Joey and Jesse didn't know they had tasted it just in time. Because these cookies were missing something. Stephanie's special secret ingredient.

"How are the cookies coming, sweetie?" Danny asked as he walked into the kitchen.

"Great," Stephanie said. "I baked one batch already. Now this batch is almost ready for the final touch."

Danny peeked into the bowl. "Really? That batter looks perfect to me."

"I suppose you want to taste it too?" Stephanie asked.

"Of course not," Danny said. "I prefer my cookies *cooked*." He reached over and snatched a cookie off the cooling rack.

"Dad, wait!" Stephanie said.

But Danny had already popped the cookie into his mouth. As he chewed, a disgusted look spread over his face. He grabbed a glass, poured in cold water, and took a deep drink.

"What is wrong with these cookies?" he cried. "What's that awful taste?" he asked.

"Chili sauce," Stephanie answered, trying not to laugh.

"Chili sauce?" Joey sent a worried glance toward the cooling rack.

"That's a pretty weird special ingredient," Jesse added.

Stephanie fought to keep a straight face. "You're right, Dad. I was just, uh, trying something new."

Danny seemed confused, but he patted Stephanie on the back. "All great chefs do that," he told her. "And just because your cookies didn't come out perfectly, that doesn't mean you should give up."

"Right," Jesse agreed.

"Right," Joey added.

"Oh, I won't give up," Stephanie told them. Because her dad was wrong about *this*. Judging from his reaction, her special-ingredient cookies were perfect. Perfect for a bunch of Flamingoes!

"Darcy, what's wrong? You look exhausted," Stephanie said. She stared at Darcy's half-open eyes as she, Allie, and Darcy headed toward Stephanie's locker. "Rough day at school?" Stephanie asked.

"No, I'm just tired," Darcy answered. She covered an enormous yawn with one hand. "I stayed up half the night working on my dress."

Allie shook her head, smiling. "Didn't you say

that dress would take only twenty minutes to make?'' she asked.

Darcy nodded. "I guess it took longer because it was my first one. But the important thing is that I finished it!''

Stephanie gaped at her in surprise. "Really? That's still pretty fast, Darce!''

"So, how does it look?'' Allie asked.

"Good—I *think*," Darcy answered. "I didn't really try it on last night. I just kind of held it up to me in front of the mirror. So, maybe you guys could come by and give me your opinions.''

"Sure," Allie agreed.

They stopped in front of Stephanie's locker and Stephanie dug out Cynthia's algebra book—and an enormous container of her special-ingredient cookies.

"Sounds like fun," Stephanie said to Darcy. "But first I have to drop these cookies off at the Flamingo bake sale.''

"How much longer are you going to let Cynthia push you around?'' Allie asked.

Stephanie frowned. "I'm not exactly letting her do that," she said. She explained about the cookies, and the special chili sauce.

Allie gasped and Darcy laughed out loud. "Good for you," Darcy told Stephanie. "It's sneaky, but it will get the Flamingoes in trouble. Anyone who buys those cookies will be furious!"

"I know." Stephanie smiled as she led the way down the front hall to the bake sale. The Flamingoes had covered a long table with a bright pink tablecloth. Lots of kids—mostly boys—were hanging around, talking and eating.

Cynthia spotted Stephanie coming and motioned frantically for Stephanie to follow her into a nearby doorway. Darcy and Allie waited at the table.

"Where have you been?" Cynthia demanded.

"I got here as soon as I could," Stephanie told her.

"Well, you should have gotten here earlier!" Cynthia said. "Rene might have noticed that my cookies weren't here yet."

Stephanie rolled her eyes. "Gee, Cynthia, I'd hate to see you get in trouble with Big Bird."

"Very funny," Cynthia said. "Come on, hand over the goods."

Stephanie handed Cynthia the tub of cookies. "Thanks," Cynthia said. Then she looked up, and turned pale. Stephanie turned around—and found herself face-to-face with Rene.

"What's going on here?" Rene demanded.

"Oh, nothing!" Cynthia smiled. "I'd better get back to the bake sale."

Rene put out a hand to stop her. "Not so fast, Cynthia. Why did Stephanie just give you those cookies?"

Cynthia shot Stephanie a desperate look. "Don't be silly, Rene," Cynthia said. "Stephanie gave them *back* to me. She wanted to taste them, but I said no. I made these for you. From scratch. I know you don't like those ones from a roll."

Cynthia pried the lid off the container and held it out to Rene. "Here—try one."

Rene helped herself to a cookie and took a big bite. She chewed. A pained expression crossed her face. She spat the half-chewed cookie into her hand.

"What are you trying to do—poison me?" Rene demanded.

"No! I—" Cynthia started to say.

Rene pushed past her and ran for the drinking fountain. Stephanie burst out laughing.

Cynthia took a tiny bite of a cookie. "Yuck!" she cried. "What did you do, Stephanie?" Her eyes widened in horror. "You're in big trouble now," she told her.

"Big deal. So Rene doesn't like my cooking," Stephanie replied. "She'll get over it."

"But I won't!" Cynthia cried. "What if Rene kicks me out of the Flamingoes for this?"

Stephanie shrugged. "It's only a cookie. That's not such a big deal, Cynthia."

"It is to me," Cynthia insisted. "So—say you're sorry."

"What do you mean?" Stephanie asked.

"You know. Kiss my feet," Cynthia ordered.

Stephanie swallowed hard. "Here? Now?" she asked.

"Right now," Cynthia demanded. "In front of everyone!"

Stephanie looked around the hallway. It was swarming with kids. "I won't do it," she said.

Cynthia's eyebrows shot up. "Do it!"

"No," Stephanie said even louder.

"I'll tell," Cynthia warned her. "I'll tell all about you-know-who!"

Stephanie took a deep breath. *This is it*, she told herself. *Either I give in, and let Cynthia push me around forever, or—*

"Listen up, everybody! I've got something to say!" Stephanie shouted as loudly as she could. Allie and Darcy gaped at her. The kids standing nearby turned to stare.

Stephanie squeezed her eyes shut and shouted: "I went out with a sixth-grader!"

CHAPTER
11

◆ ◀ ◆ ◆

"What did I do?" Stephanie moaned. She and Allie were sprawled across Darcy's bed. They had rushed to Darcy's after school to see her dress. Darcy was changing into it now in the bathroom.

"I still can't believe I told. Now everyone knows my deepest secret!" Stephanie frowned.

"It was pretty amazing," Allie said. "But Cynthia really pushed you too far."

"You're right. I couldn't take it anymore." Stephanie stared up at the ceiling. "But now I feel like I'm about to be hit by a train and there's nothing I can do to stop it."

"What do you think will happen when you walk into the dance with Dixon?" Allie asked.

Stephanie groaned. "I *can't* take him to the dance now! I'd die of embarrassment."

"So what are you going to do?" Allie asked.

"Dump him," Stephanie said. "And then I'll tell everyone I *stopped* dating him the minute I found out how old he was."

"That could work," Allie admitted.

The bathroom door swung open. "Please don't laugh," Darcy said quickly. She hesitated, then marched into the room and turned around, modeling the dress. "It's a disaster, isn't it?" she asked in a tearful voice.

Stephanie bit her lip. "Well, not a *total* disaster," she said.

"I'm sure we can fix it," Allie added.

Stephanie and Allie looked at each other helplessly. Darcy's dress looked awful. The hem was totally uneven. The left sleeve was so tight Darcy couldn't bend her arm at the elbow. The right sleeve was droopy and baggy.

Darcy collapsed onto the bed. She blinked hard and a few tears spilled down her cheeks.

Stephanie scooted closer to her. "Don't cry, Darce," she said, patting her on the back. "It's not *that* bad. Uh—the color is really pretty."

"But I—worked so—hard!" Darcy drew in a shaky breath.

"I just know we can fix it. I know!" Allie said. "You could cut the bottom part off and then make a new hem that's straight," she suggested. "And, uh—"

"And you could make that loose sleeve tighter—" Stephanie added.

"No! Cut them *both* off and make short sleeves!" Allie exclaimed.

Darcy started crying even harder. "I thought I was done!" she wailed. She flopped facedown on her bed. "I just want to be alone, okay?"

Allie and Stephanie tiptoed out of Darcy's room. They headed toward the front door.

"Do you think she can fix the dress?" Allie asked.

Stephanie shook her head. "I don't think even *Amanda Wong* could fix that dress!"

Stephanie left Allie on Allie's corner and hurried the rest of the way home. D.J. looked up from the kitchen table.

"Hey, Steph—your turn to help set the table."

"Okay." Stephanie opened the refrigerator, pulled out the water, and poured herself a big drink.

"Oh—Dixon called you earlier," D.J. said. "He

wanted to know what time to pick you up on Saturday night."

"I'm not going with him," Stephanie told her. "Everyone at school knows how old he is now. Going with him would just be too embarrassing."

D.J. looked up in surprise. "But the dance is this weekend. You'd better tell him you're breaking the date—and *soon*," she said.

"But I don't know what to say," Stephanie admitted.

"Just tell him the truth. That always works best," D.J. advised.

Stephanie sighed. "Can I use the phone in your bedroom, Deej?" she asked.

"Sure," D.J. said with a smile. "And good luck."

"Thanks, I'll need it." Stephanie slowly dragged herself up the stairs. She let herself into D.J.'s room, sat down on the bed, and pulled the phone onto her lap. *You can do this!* she told herself. She quickly dialed Dixon's number before she lost her nerve.

Brring! Brring!

He's not answering! Stephanie thought. *Maybe I should just hang up. I could always call back later. Like when I'm in college.*

Brring! Click.

"Hey, this is Dixon. I'm not here right now. You know what to do." *Beep*.

Stephanie blinked in surprise. Dixon had his own phone line, and his own *answering machine?* He was so lucky!

"Uh, hi, Dixon, it's Stephanie. . . ."

She paused. What should she say next?

"Uh, about the dance," she began. "Well, the thing is, I don't think we should go together. I—uh, I don't want to see you anymore. You're a really nice guy, and our dates were really fun. But it's just that—uh, I think you're too young for me. So. Anyway. Okay. Bye now. Thanks."

She quickly hung up. Her face was burning. *I sounded like a total idiot!* she thought.

Oh, who cares? The important thing was she had done it. She had broken the date with Dixon!

She had to tell Allie and Darcy. The phone rang in her father's office. She ran to pick it up. "Hello?" she snapped.

"Is that you, Stephanie?"

Dixon!

"Oh! Uh, uh, hi," Stephanie sputtered.

"Hey—what's going on? I walked in while you were recording your message," Dixon said. "What kind of person breaks up with an answering machine? That stinks!"

"Well, I, uh, thought it would be easier on you that way," Stephanie said. "You know, because girls are more mature than boys and—"

"You're such a chicken!" Dixon told her. "I may be younger than you, but *you're* the one who's acting immature!"

"I am not!" Stephanie shouted. She slammed down the phone and started to pace the room.

What nerve! she thought. *How dare he call me back that way!*

"Steph?" D.J. peeked into her room. "How did it go?"

"Fine. Great!" Stephanie said. "No—oh, D.J., it was awful!" she added. "He sounded so hurt, and angry."

D.J. hurried over and put her arm around Stephanie. "Don't feel too bad," she said. "He'll get over it."

"But I'm not sure *I* will," Stephanie confessed. "I'm so confused! You and Becky and Allie told me not to dump him!"

Stephanie rushed into her own room. She slammed the door, kicked off her shoes, and dove under the covers of her bed.

"Stephanie!" The door flew open and Michelle barged into the room. "Dad says dinner is ready."

"Tell him I'm not hungry," Stephanie said. "My stomach hurts."

Michelle peered closely at her. "You're crying! Did you have a fight with Darcy or Allie?"

"No," Stephanie said. "With Dixon." When she said his name, the tears started flowing. "Michelle, you go down to dinner. I could use some time alone."

"Okay," Michelle agreed. She turned at the door. "I think you should just call him and say you're sorry."

Stephanie stared at the door after Michelle left. Things were so easy when you were nine. There was no way a simple phone call could solve *this* problem.

CHAPTER
12

♦ ◂ ◆ ♦

"Hey, Stephanie!" Mary Kelly called out. "I have an idea for you!"

Stephanie ignored Mary as she climbed onto the bus the next morning.

"Why don't you take my little brother to the dance? Or is six too old for you?" Mary burst out laughing.

A few kids sitting near her laughed too. And Stephanie heard other kids whispering as she walked down the aisle of the bus.

Stephanie felt her cheeks burn. *Here it comes,* she thought. *But I can't let anyone think it bothers me.*

Stephanie stopped by Mary's seat and flashed her a brilliant smile. "Mary, if your brother looks anything like you, I'm really not interested," she said.

"Good one!" Ronnie Perkins called out. His friends hooted.

Stephanie slipped into a seat behind Darcy and Allie. "Sorry, you guys," she muttered. "I bet you're embarrassed to be seen with me."

"As if!" Darcy rolled her eyes. "Who cares what they think anyway?"

"Sure. Besides, if Dixon were older than you, nobody would think twice about it," Allie said. "Right?"

"Right," Stephanie agreed.

Allie had a good point. Stephanie began to relax. Maybe things wouldn't be so bad after all. Then the bus reached school and Stephanie walked into the front hall. A whole group of Flamingoes was waiting for her.

"Wah, wah, wah!" Rene cried, doing an impression of a screaming baby. Darah Judson and Cynthia sucked their thumbs. The rest of the Flamingoes hooted and jeered, making baby noises. Everyone near them cracked up.

Don't let them get to you, Stephanie told herself.

"Oh, look, Stephanie," Darcy called out. "None of Rene's friends ever stopped sucking their thumbs!"

"Yeah, I wonder if they still wear diapers too," Allie loudly added.

Allie and Darcy laughed out loud—and so did a bunch of kids walking by. Stephanie forced herself to laugh along with them. But she could feel her face burning again. She wished she could disappear.

The rest of the day didn't go much better. She practically raced into first-period English class. She felt sure she'd be safe in her favorite class. But as soon as she sat down, someone behind her started to whistle.

Then another whistler joined in. And then another. Stephanie recognized the tune. It was "Rock-a-Bye, Baby."

She put her head down and groaned. So much for feeling safe!

One class down, six to go, Stephanie told herself. Geometry was next. She entered the room with her head held high. Everyone was watching her, but she pretended not to notice. She swung into her seat—and popped back up.

"Ouch!" she cried out. "What was that?" She stared at her chair. A baby rattle lay there. The whole class started laughing.

Stephanie shoved the rattle into the bottom of

her backpack. "What a great gift!" she said out loud. "I'll give it to my neighbor's new baby!"

The laughing quieted finally. But then it was time for earth science class.

"You're late, Stephanie," Mr. Signorelli said as Stephanie hurried into the room.

"Sorry," Stephanie said. She had been hiding in the girls' room until it was time to come in. She examined her chair and carefully sat down.

"Today is Thursday—group project day," Mr. Signorelli announced. "Everybody choose up partners."

"Want to be my partner?"

Stephanie looked up. Kyle Sullivan was standing next to her desk.

"Sure," Stephanie said in surprise. Kyle pulled a chair close to Stephanie's. He looked as cute as ever with his blond hair curling against his neck and his deep brown eyes.

"How come you're talking to me?" Stephanie asked Kyle. "I thought you were still mad about the ski trip—you know, when I told everyone about your middle name."

"After today, I guess I feel like we're even," Kyle said. "Everyone is teasing you just like everyone teased me about being called Rufus."

"Sorry! Now I know how it feels—bad," Stephanie told him.

Kyle leaned closer to Stephanie. "I think this whole fuss about you dating a younger guy is stupid."

Stephanie stared at him. "Really?"

"Sure," Kyle said. "I mean, think about it. If I dated a seventh-grade girl, nobody would make fun of me. Why shouldn't you date a boy two years younger than you?"

"I'm surprised you feel that way," Stephanie admitted. "You have kind of—uh, old-fashioned ideas about dating," she went on.

"Maybe," Kyle admitted. "But I think it's cool that *you* don't. You date whoever you like."

"And you should also get busy on your project before the class is over." Mr. Signorelli stood over them.

"We're getting to work right now," Kyle told him.

Stephanie was ready to think about earth science. Thinking about her life was way too confusing.

"I'm so glad you guys are here!" Darcy exclaimed. She flung open the front door to her house. It was Friday evening—only one day before the "Girls Rule" dance.

108

"I fixed my whole dress," Darcy told them. "I can't wait to show it to you!"

Stephanie and Allie followed Darcy up the stairs. "Ta-da!" Darcy threw open the door to her bedroom.

Stephanie stared at the beautiful dress lying on Darcy's bed. "It looks perfect!" she said.

"I took your advice," Darcy said. "I made it shorter and I cut off the sleeves."

"Let's see how it looks on you," Allie said.

"Okay!" Darcy snatched the dress off the bed and hurried into the bathroom. A few minutes later, the door opened and Darcy waltzed out, swinging her hips like a model on a runway.

"Isn't it fabulous?" she asked.

"Well . . ." Stephanie mumbled. "It looked good *off*."

Darcy studied her reflection in the mirror on her door. "It looks fine *on* too," she insisted.

"Why does the fabric bunch up over your stomach?" Allie asked.

"I don't know!" Darcy exclaimed. "But if I hold my hands in front of my waist, you can't even see it."

"It will be pretty hard to dance that way," Stephanie said.

Darcy's shoulders slumped. "Okay—I admit it! This is the ugliest dress I've ever seen!"

"Why don't you wear that red dress you bought for your aunt's wedding last year?" Stephanie suggested.

"She's right," Allie agreed. "The dance is *tomorrow* night, Darce. You should be ready by now."

"Well, Stephanie isn't ready," Darcy pointed out. "She doesn't even have a date!"

"That's right!" Allie gasped. "Stephanie, you'd better call my cousin Gus right this minute!"

"I'm not taking Gus," Stephanie protested. "I'd rather stay home."

"You have to call someone!" Allie exclaimed. "I know—call Kyle!"

Stephanie groaned. "I can't. Kyle thinks I'm really cool for dating Dixon!"

"So, fib!" Darcy suggested. "Tell Kyle that Dixon had to leave town suddenly."

"Kyle would definitely *not* buy that." Stephanie shook her head. "Forget it."

"No way!" Allie wailed. "I really want you to be there!"

"The dance won't be fun without you," Darcy agreed.

"Not true. You guys will have tons of fun. And I don't mind staying home. Because there's no way I'm going tomorrow night," Stephanie insisted. "And that's final!"

CHAPTER
13

◆ ◂ ◂ ◆

Stephanie stared at the TV, trying to watch an old Jerry Lewis movie. She glanced at her watch. Four o'clock. In only three and a half more hours, Allie and Darcy would be meeting their dates and heading to the "Girls Rule" dance.

Stephanie gave a loud sigh. Joey stopped in his tracks on his way out the front door.

"Steph, for the last time—please come to the CD store with me," he begged.

"No thanks." Stephanie answered without taking her eyes off the screen. "There's another movie on right after this one. I don't want to miss it."

"But you've been moping around the house all

day," Joey said. "You're beginning to scare Comet," he joked.

Comet heard his name and looked up and whined. Stephanie patted his head.

"Come on, Steph," Joey pleaded. "I can't stand to see you this way. And remember, whatever I buy to play at the dance becomes part of my permanent collection. Are you sure you want me to pick them out myself?"

Joey made a silly face. Stephanie grinned. "Oh, okay," she said. "I give up. I'll come."

"Great! Joey grabbed his car keys and Stephanie followed him outside. In no time they were at the mall. When they reached the CD store, Joey headed straight for the discount bin.

"Hey, here's a good one! New Kids on the Block. They're pretty happening, aren't they?"

Stephanie rolled her eyes. "Joey, even those guys' *mothers* don't listen to them anymore. If you want decent music, you're going to have to pay full price."

Joey stuck out his lower lip. He put the New Kids CD back. "Well, what would you suggest?"

"Looking through another bin," Stephanie said. She headed across the store. "How about this new . . ." Her voice trailed off. Dixon was standing practically across from her.

Yikes! She gulped. She considered hiding, but it was too late. Dixon was staring right at her. Even Joey noticed him.

"Uh-oh," he said. "Isn't that the guy you gave the old heave-ho?"

Stephanie nodded.

"I think I'll check out the easy-listening section," Joey said, backing away.

Stephanie swallowed hard. Dixon crossed the aisle. "Hi," he said.

"Uh, hi." Stephanie felt her heart thudding in her chest.

Dixon glanced away nervously. "Listen, I'm sorry I called you a chicken," he said. "Sometimes when I'm mad I say things I don't really mean."

"I'm the one who should apologize," Stephanie told him. "I'm really sorry. You were right on the phone. You did act more mature than me."

Dixon brushed his hair away from his eyes and grinned. "Really? Mature enough to go to the dance with you?"

Stephanie smiled. "You'd still go with me?"

"Sure. If *you* want to," Dixon said.

"Yeah. I guess I really want to!" Stephanie exclaimed.

"Then we have a date," Dixon said.

"Great!" Stephanie said. "So, I'll see you around seven-thirty. Okay?"

"Okay," Dixon said. "See you later."

Stephanie watched Dixon head for the cash register. She glanced at her watch. Four-thirty! Her stomach jumped about a foot. She had only three hours to get ready for the dance—and she had absolutely nothing to wear!

"Hey, I hear you're going to the dance," D.J. said.

Stephanie turned away from her closet. "I'm supposed to. But, D.J.—I can't find anything to wear!"

"Maybe that's because there's nothing left in your closet," D.J. said. She looked around the room and shook her head.

Clothes were piled everywhere. Stephanie's bed was covered. Michelle's bed was covered. Tops and skirts were strewn over both desks and there were belts, purses, and shoes scattered over the floor.

"Please—don't bug me about the mess now!" Stephanie wailed. "Allie's mom's coming to pick me up in half an hour! What am I going to do?"

She leaned over and picked a sweater up off the floor. "Why didn't I buy a dress when Allie did? I have *nothing* to wear. Nothing!"

"Okay, okay, don't panic," D.J. told her. "Let's

be calm. First, we need to get rid of these tops and skirts. They're not nearly dressy enough for tonight. Then we can see what we have to work with."

"Good plan," Stephanie agreed. "You put those aside, and I'll pile all my dresses on Michelle's bed."

For the next few minutes Stephanie and D.J. sorted through the mounds of clothes. Finally, they had all the dresses spread out on the bed. D.J. frowned at the selection.

"Too casual, too casual," she said, picking up two dresses and flinging them onto Stephanie's bed. "How about this pink one? It's pretty dressy."

"No way! I can't wear pink. I'll look like a Flamingo!" Stephanie told her.

"Well, what about this blue one?" D.J. asked.

"The waist is too tight. I wouldn't be able to move all night," Stephanie said.

D.J. looked grim. "You're right, Steph. You have nothing."

Stephanie felt her heart sink.

"Wait! I have an idea!" D.J. grabbed Stephanie's hand. "Come on."

"Where are we going?" Stephanie asked.

"To my room," D.J. said. "I think I have a dress that will be just right."

D.J. dragged Stephanie down the hall. D.J. pulled a black linen sundress out of her closet. "Put this on," she ordered.

"That? I'll look like I'm going to a boring grownup dinner," Stephanie protested.

"It's a sundress," D.J. explained. "It's very bare in back. Trust me," D.J. said. "This dress is very sophisticated."

Stephanie shrugged. She threw off her robe and quickly changed into the dress. She stood back and examined herself in the full-length mirror.

"You look fantastic," D.J. told her.

"Hey, nice outfit!" Becky peeked through the doorway. "But hang on a minute. I have the perfect finishing touch!"

Becky ran upstairs. A minute later she was back. She tossed Stephanie a pair of black, strappy high-heeled shoes. She also brought a pair of dangly gold earrings and two gold bangle bracelets.

"Put these on, Steph," she said. "They're simple, and very elegant."

Stephanie tried them on. "Perfect!" she said.

Becky eyed her sharply. "You need help with your makeup," she said. "You need a little more color to go with that dark dress."

"And let's put up your hair," D.J. suggested. "That will look more formal."

Becky added more eyeliner, some eye shadow, and blush to Stephanie's face. Finally, she brushed on a layer of hot-pink lipstick.

D.J. twisted her hair into a French braid. "Done!" she cried.

Stephanie checked out the finished look in the mirror. Her mouth dropped open.

"I look amazing!" she said. "I look tons older. At least sixteen!" She blinked at her image in amazement. She couldn't stop staring.

D.J. grinned at Becky. "I think that means she likes it," she teased.

"Seriously, Steph," Becky told her, "you look beautiful. It's a whole new look."

"I'll say," Stephanie murmured.

Downstairs, the doorbell rang.

"Yikes!" Stephanie gulped. "That must be Dixon!"

"Are you nervous?" D.J. asked.

"A little." Stephanie bit her lip.

"Don't worry about a thing. You look fantastic," Becky assured her. "Dixon will be blown away."

"Absolutely," D.J. agreed.

"Thanks so much, you guys!" Stephanie spun around in a circle, admiring herself in the mirror one last time.

"Stephanie! Dixon's here!" Danny called from downstairs.

Stephanie was suddenly glad that Joey and Jesse had already left for the dance, and that Michelle was at a sleepover. She didn't need a bigger audience than she already had. It would be hard enough to face Dixon and her father with her new look!

"Hurry, Steph. You'd better rescue Dixon before Dad gives him the third degree," D.J. said.

Stephanie's eyes widened. "You're right!" She grabbed her purse and hurried into the hallway. She paused at the top of the stairs and took a deep breath. Then she walked down the stairs, being careful to look as mature as possible.

Dixon and Danny were waiting in the front hallway. Dixon caught sight of Stephanie and he seemed a little dazed.

I guess he likes my new look, Stephanie thought with satisfaction.

Dixon looked pretty terrific himself. Stephanie hardly recognized him without jeans or shorts and a baggy T-shirt. He was wearing dark pants and a matching jacket over a tight-fitting white T-shirt. His hair was carefully smoothed back. He held tightly on to a small white box.

"Hi," Stephanie said, feeling a bit shy.

"Hi," Dixon said. "Uh, these are for you." He held out the box. Inside was a wrist corsage—small white roses.

"They're beautiful!" Stephanie cried. She slipped the corsage onto her wrist. "Thanks, Dixon."

"You're welcome," Dixon said. He swallowed. "You look . . . different," he said.

"Thanks," Stephanie told him.

Beep! Beep!

"That must be Allie and Zack!" Stephanie said. "Let's go, Dixon."

"One minute!" Danny said. "I want to get a picture first!"

Stephanie knew there was no point in arguing with her father. He wouldn't take no for an answer. "Okay, but hurry it up," she said.

"Okay, why don't you stand in front of the fireplace," Danny directed.

Stephanie hurried into place and Dixon slipped his arm around her shoulder.

Stephanie gazed up at him. She felt like Cinderella finding Prince Charming again.

Amazing, she thought. Three hours earlier, she was convinced she didn't want to go to the dance. Now she couldn't wait!

"How about a big smile?" Danny asked.

"No problem!" Stephanie answered happily.

CHAPTER
14

"There's Mrs. Powell," Stephanie said. "But where's Darcy?"

Stephanie, Allie, Dixon, and Zack stared at the front porch of Darcy's house. Stephanie and Allie were sitting next to each other in the back of the Taylors' station wagon. Dixon was on Stephanie's other side. Zack, Allie's date, was sitting up front with Allie's mom.

Darcy's mother was frantically gesturing at the girls.

"I think she wants us to come inside," Allie said.

Stephanie looked at Dixon. "I'll be right back," she said.

"Okay," Dixon answered.

The girls scrambled out of the car and hurried up to Darcy's front door.

"I'm so glad you're here!" Mrs. Powell told them. "I don't know what's wrong with Darcy. She won't come out of her room! Maybe she'll tell you what's wrong."

Allie and Stephanie looked at each other in dismay. "Now what?" Stephanie said.

They followed Mrs. Powell into the house. Justin, Darcy's date, sat on the couch in the living room. He seemed confused—and a little impatient.

"Hi, Justin," Stephanie greeted him.

"Hey," Justin replied. "Is something wrong with Darcy?"

"Uh—no," Stephanie said. "Why don't you go hang out with the other guys in the car?"

"Okay," Justin agreed. He got up and hurried toward the door.

Allie and Stephanie ran upstairs and banged on Darcy's door.

"Hey, Darcy!" Stephanie called. "Let us in!"

After a moment, Darcy unlocked the door. Stephanie and Allie rushed inside.

"What's wrong?" Stephanie asked. "You're not even dressed yet!"

Darcy was still in jeans and a T-shirt. She looked frantic.

"I'm still trying to finish my dress!" Darcy exclaimed.

"But the boys are waiting outside," Allie said.

"Darcy, you don't have time to finish. We'll miss the dance!" Stephanie told her.

"I just need a few more minutes," Darcy insisted.

"Can I help?" Stephanie asked.

"Sure," Darcy said. "Grab a needle and thread. You can help me finish the hem. It's taking forever."

Stephanie grabbed a needle and quickly threaded it. For once she was glad that Danny had taught her how to sew. Sewing a hem couldn't be much more complicated than sewing on a button.

Allie also grabbed a needle. They both began stitching.

"Girls!" Mrs. Powell yelled from the other side of the door. "What is going on in there?"

"We'll be out in a minute!" Darcy shouted.

Stephanie started to make her stitches bigger—much bigger.

"Done!" she said.

"Me too," Allie cried.

"Great!" Darcy pulled off her T-shirt and jeans and slipped on the dress.

Stephanie gasped. The new hem was finally straight. But the dress was also short. *Very* short.

"How does it look?" Darcy turned to see herself in the full-length mirror.

Stephanie couldn't help herself. She started to giggle. "You can't go to the dance in that. You'll be kicked out!"

"Or arrested!" Allie said. She started laughing.

Darcy stared at her reflection. "Oh, no!" she groaned. "This dress is so short, it's practically a *shirt!*"

Stephanie nodded. "You're right. It's tunic-length now. It would look great with black leggings."

Darcy started to smile. "Hey—why not? That's a great idea!" She ran to her dresser and yanked out a pair of leggings. She pulled them on under the bright blue dress, then added a pair of black high heels.

"Well?" Darcy asked.

She turned around. The blue dress—as a tunic—looked suddenly chic and sophisticated. And the black leggings and shoes gave it just the right touch.

"Well, it's not exactly a long, formal dress like you wanted," Stephanie pointed out.

"But it is kind of glamorous in its own way," Allie added.

"Yeah, it's actually pretty cool," Stephanie agreed.

"I like it!" Darcy decided. "It's one of a kind."

"It's definitely that," Stephanie said.

Darcy broke into a relieved smile. "See? I told you I could make my own dress."

"Your own tunic, you mean," Stephanie corrected her.

Darcy laughed.

"I wonder what Amanda Wong would say?" Allie asked.

"Probably that making a dress will be easier the second time," Stephanie replied.

"No way!" Darcy shook her head. "There won't *be* a second time. I'm hanging up my needle and thread. Sewing is much too much work. Shopping is a lot more fun!"

Darcy combed out her hair and quickly dabbed on makeup.

"You look great, Darce," Stephanie told her. "Now let's get outside—before our dates give up and go to the dance without us," Stephanie said.

Fifteen minutes later they entered the school gym—with their dates.

"This place looks terrific!" Stephanie exclaimed in amazement.

"I hardly recognize the place," Allie agreed.

The decorating committee had done an incredible job. Hundreds of bright balloons floated against the high ceiling. Huge panels of silver cloth were draped over the walls, hiding the bare wood.

Round tables covered with gleaming silver tablecloths filled half of the huge room. Bowls of pale flowers sat in the middle of each table, trimmed with silver ribbons.

"It's gorgeous," Darcy said.

The gym was packed with kids. A few couples were already out on the dance floor.

"Hey—there are Jesse and Joey," Allie said.

They had set up their equipment on the stage. Stephanie was relieved to see that they were wearing normal clothes—dark pants and jackets with dark blue shirts. But best of all, the song they were playing was one of Stephanie's favorites.

"Let's grab some chairs," Darcy suggested, pointing to a nearby table.

"Good idea!" Justin said. He grabbed some chairs—and held them up in the air. "Now what?" he joked.

Darcy stared at him. "I mean, let's find a table before they're all taken," she said.

"Only kidding," Justin said. He set the chairs back on the floor.

Everyone started to sit down when a fast song started playing.

"Hey, that's one of my favorite songs to dance to," Stephanie told Dixon. "Let's go!"

"Are you guys coming?" she asked the others.

"I guess we *should* dance," Justin joked. "After all, they don't call this a *sit*."

Darcy groaned.

"But, let's wait awhile, okay?" Justin told Darcy. "I want something to drink first." Justin headed toward the refreshment table without waiting for Darcy to answer.

Darcy trailed after him. Stephanie could tell she was disappointed.

Zack and Allie headed for the dance floor. Dixon and Stephanie followed them.

They started dancing. Dixon was a great dancer, Stephanie thought. Not too wild, but not too up-tight either.

The fast song ended and a slow one came on. Stephanie stepped closer to Dixon. He slipped his arms around her waist and Stephanie rested her hands on his shoulders.

"Check out Darcy and Justin," Dixon said.

Stephanie glanced back toward their table. Darcy

waited for Justin to gulp down his drink. Then she dragged him onto the dance floor. She started to put her arms on his shoulders, but Justin danced away from her, fooling around.

"Poor Darcy," Stephanie murmured. So much for Darcy's super-mature ninth-grade date. Finally, Justin settled down and moved closer to Darcy. But he locked his elbows and held her as far away as possible. Stephanie shot Darcy a sympathetic look. She hoped Justin would settle down before the night was over.

"Hey, look—your friend from the movies is here," Dixon told Stephanie.

She glanced around in surprise. "What friend?"

Dixon pointed. Cynthia! Stephanie stared. Cynthia was standing with her date, a boy in the seventh grade. Stephanie couldn't believe what he was wearing: a bright green tuxedo with a matching bow tie.

Stephanie sneaked a grateful glance at Dixon. Thank goodness he had better taste in clothes than that!

Cynthia caught Stephanie's eye. Cynthia stuck her thumb in her mouth and pretended to cry. Stephanie shrugged. Cynthia's teasing didn't bother her anymore. She was at the dance with a really great guy—and that was all that mattered.

"What is she doing?" Dixon asked, looking confused.

"Who knows?" Stephanie said. "Sometimes she really acts like a baby!"

When the song was over, Dixon went to get them both something to drink. Stephanie headed back to their table—and bumped right into Rene. Naturally, she was wearing a bright pink dress.

Stephanie nodded at her politely. "Hi, Rene. Having fun?"

"Sure," Rene said. "I always have fun with Kyle."

"Kyle?" Stephanie tried not to sound as surprised as she felt. "You asked Kyle to the dance?"

"Of course," Rene told her. "Did you think he'd want to go with you?" Rene smirked. "Kyle prefers to date girls his own age, you know."

"Well, I just like to date tall, cute boys—no matter how old they are," Stephanie told her.

Rene shrugged and walked away. Stephanie smiled. *I handled her all right*, she thought. She turned to go back to her table and saw Dixon standing right next to her.

Dixon gave her a funny look. "What did all that stuff about age mean anyway?" he asked.

Stephanie felt herself flush. "Well, you know. Some girls make a big deal out of ages. Personally,

I couldn't care less that you're only in the sixth grade."

"Well, what grade are you in anyway?" Dixon asked her.

Uh-oh, she thought. *Here it is—the moment I've been dreading.*

"Uh, what grade do you think I'm in?" Stephanie asked him, stalling.

Dixon shrugged. "I don't know. Seventh, I guess."

"That's close," Stephanie said, smiling.

Dixon frowned. "I don't get it. What grade *are* you in?"

Stephanie paused. "Eighth," she blurted out.

Dixon gaped at her. "How old are you?"

"I—I'm thirteen," Stephanie told him.

Dixon looked stunned for a moment. "Wow!" he finally said. "I thought you looked pretty grown-up tonight, but . . ." He trailed off.

"Does it matter to you?" Stephanie finally asked. "Because my friend Mackenzie is having a party next Friday. I thought you might want to come."

"Well, I—" Dixon coughed. "I don't think that's a good idea. I don't think we should see each other anymore."

Stephanie couldn't believe what she was hearing. "What—why not?"

"Well, it's your friends," Dixon told her.

"What's wrong with my friends?" Stephanie asked.

"Darcy kept us waiting for half an hour," Dixon said. "And that guy Justin acts like a real jerk. He's over in the corner right now, throwing spitballs."

Stephanie cringed. She had to admit Justin *was* acting like a jerk. "But at least Justin is in the ninth grade!" she protested.

Dixon shrugged. "Well, what about your friend Cynthia, sucking her thumb?"

"She was only kidding around," Stephanie argued.

Dixon shook his head. "I'm sorry, Stephanie," he said. "Older or not, your friends are so immature."

Stephanie stared at him in disbelief. "If that's how you feel, I guess this is it, then," she said.

Dixon leaned over and gave her a quick kiss on the cheek. "We can still be friends, can't we?" he asked.

Stephanie stared at him for a moment. She didn't know whether to be insulted or angry—or what. Then Dixon started to smile, and she had to smile along with him.

"I guess so," she agreed. "As friends, we have a pretty good time together."

"So, I'll give you a call soon," Dixon said.

"Maybe we'll catch another movie. And if you don't have a date, Mackenzie's party could be fun."

"Why not?" Stephanie said. She held out her hand. "Friends?" she asked.

"Friends," Dixon answered.

Stephanie opened the front door and drifted into the living room. D.J. was curled up on the couch with her biology textbook. Danny was poring over an enormous Amanda Wong cookbook, *Everything You Always Wanted to Know about Appetizers.*

Danny glanced up. "Hi, honey! You're right on time. How was the dance?"

"Perfect," Stephanie said.

D.J.'s eyes grew round. *"Perfect?"*

"Well, almost." Stephanie flopped down on the couch next to D.J. "Except that mature ninth-grader Justin acted like a dork the entire evening."

"Poor Darcy," D.J. said.

Stephanie smiled. "She was fine. After a while she just started dancing with this guy Ken from her English class."

"How was Allie's date?" Danny asked.

"Zack was fun." Stephanie grinned. "He and Allie and Dixon and I had our own mini dance contest. Dixon and I won!"

"So, you and Dixon had a good time?" Danny asked.

"The best," Stephanie said. "Dixon is really nice. And very mature for his age. After all, not many guys would completely forgive me for acting like such a jerk."

"Well, I think you learned a valuable lesson tonight," Danny said.

"I did?" Stephanie made a face. "I thought I was just having a good time."

"Well, you learned that age doesn't always matter," Danny said. "In the long run, what matters more is *character*."

Stephanie nodded. "You're right. The next time a great guy crashes into my life, I'm not going to get so frazzled about how old he is. But, Dad, I think *you* learned a lesson too."

"I did?" Danny asked with a frown.

"Sure," Stephanie said. She imitated Danny's best lecturing voice. "You learned that long hair and earrings don't matter. Character matters!"

D.J. started to laugh and, before long, Danny joined in. "Okay, Stephanie," he said. "You win! So I guess this proves that sometimes even a younger person can teach an older person a valuable lesson."

"Dad, you've got that right!" Stephanie grinned.

It doesn't matter if you live around the corner...
or around the world...
If you are a fan of Mary-Kate and Ashley Olsen,
you should be a member of

MARY-KATE + ASHLEY'S FUN CLUB™

Here's what you get:
Our Funzine™
An autographed color photo
Two black & white individual photos
A full size color poster
An official **Fun Club**™ membership card
A **Fun Club**™ school folder
Two special **Fun Club**™ surprises
A holiday card
Fun Club™ collectibles catalog
Plus a **Fun Club**™ box to keep everything in

To join Mary-Kate + Ashley's Fun Club™, fill out the form
below and send it along with

U.S. Residents – $17.00
Canadian Residents – $22 U.S. Funds
International Residents – $27 U.S. Funds

MARY-KATE + ASHLEY'S FUN CLUB™
859 HOLLYWOOD WAY, SUITE 275
BURBANK, CA 91505

NAME:_____

ADDRESS:_____

_CITY:_____ STATE:_____ ZIP:_____

PHONE:(____) _____ BIRTHDATE:_____

1242

FULL HOUSE™
Stephanie

PHONE CALL FROM A FLAMINGO	88004-7/$3.99
THE BOY-OH-BOY NEXT DOOR	88121-3/$3.99
TWIN TROUBLES	88290-2/$3.99
HIP HOP TILL YOU DROP	88291-0/$3.99
HERE COMES THE BRAND NEW ME	89858-2/$3.99
THE SECRET'S OUT	89859-0/$3.99
DADDY'S NOT-SO-LITTLE GIRL	89860-4/$3.99
P.S. FRIENDS FOREVER	89861-2/$3.99
GETTING EVEN WITH THE FLAMINGOES	52273-6/$3.99
THE DUDE OF MY DREAMS	52274-4/$3.99
BACK-TO-SCHOOL COOL	52275-2/$3.99
PICTURE ME FAMOUS	52276-0/$3.99
TWO-FOR-ONE CHRISTMAS FUN	53546-3/$3.99
THE BIG FIX-UP MIX-UP	53547-1/$3.99
TEN WAYS TO WRECK A DATE	53548-X/$3.99
WISH UPON A VCR	53549-8/$3.99
DOUBLES OR NOTHING	56841-8/$3.99
SUGAR AND SPICE ADVICE	56842-6/$3.99
NEVER TRUST A FLAMINGO	56843-4/$3.99
THE TRUTH ABOUT BOYS	00361-5/$3.99

FULL HOUSE™
Michelle

#1: THE GREAT PET PROJECT 51905-0/$3.50

#2: THE SUPER-DUPER SLEEPOVER PARTY
51906-9/$3.50

#3: MY TWO BEST FRIENDS 52271-X/$3.50

#4: LUCKY, LUCKY DAY 52272-8/$3.50

#5: THE GHOST IN MY CLOSET 53573-0/$3.99

#6: BALLET SURPRISE 53574-9/$3.99

#7: MAJOR LEAGUE TROUBLE 53575-7/$3.50

#8: MY FOURTH-GRADE MESS 53576-5/$3.99

#9: BUNK 3, TEDDY, AND ME 56834-5/$3.50

#10: MY BEST FRIEND IS A MOVIE STAR!
(Super Edition) 56835-3/$3.50

#11: THE BIG TURKEY ESCAPE 56836-1/$3.50

#12: THE SUBSTITUTE TEACHER 00364-X/$3.50

A MINSTREL® BOOK
Published by Pocket Books

Simon & Schuster Mail Order Dept. BWB
200 Old Tappan Rd., Old Tappan, N.J. 07675

Please send me the books I have checked above. I am enclosing $_____(please add $0.75 to cover the postage and handling for each order. Please add appropriate sales tax). Send check or money order--no cash or C.O.D.'s please. Allow up to six weeks for delivery. For purchase over $10.00 you may use VISA: card number, expiration date and customer signature must be included.

Name _____

Address _____

City _____ State/Zip _____

VISA Card # _____ Exp.Date _____

Signature _____

1033-15